Broken Waters

By Frank L. Packard

First published in 1925

Stillwoods Edition, 2020
Stillwoods.Blogspot.Ca

Catalogue Information:
Title: Broken Waters
Author: Frank L. Packard (1877-1942)
First published in England, Canada and USA, 1925.
This Edition by: Stillwoods, 2020, (Doug Frizzle)
ISBN Canada: 978-1-989788-01-1
Blog: Stillwoods.Blogspot.Ca
Author Blog: https://franklpackard.blogspot.com/
Storefront: http://www.lulu.com/spotlight/lulubook22

Keywords: Frank Packard, mystery, thriller

Paris Underworld, Spell of the Tropics, Mystery and Adventure
The scenes of this thrilling story vary from Havre and Paris, to the romantic islands of Polynesia, where the last threads of the plots are finally untangled.

John Crane, a middle-aged man of wealth and adventure, is asleep on his ocean-going yacht in the Port of Havre, when he is unduly awakened in the wee small hours of the morning upon the insistance of an Englishman, just arrived from Paris by motor.

The Englishman reveals himself as a friend of Martin Todd, an old pal of Crane's, who has agreed to help a group of Russian Noblemen in an endeavor to smuggle some valuable jewels out of Russia.

Crane, of course, is eager to accept the jewels and guard them, although he is warned that Soviet agents will cause trouble. And thus the plot is launched.

Next the scene shifts to the Paris Underworld, where Anne Walton, the daughter of a rich planter, is discovered on an errand of mercy.

A gripping, hair-raising story.

FRANK L. PACKARD

AUTHOR OF

"Running Special," "The Locked Book," "Adventures of Jimmie Dale," "The Beloved Traitor," "The Doors of the Night," "The Four Stragglers," "From Now On," "Pawned," "Wire Devils," "Greater Love Hath No Man," etc.

Stillwoods Editions are a poor complement to some great stories and authors. Doug Frizzle is 'Stillwoods'; in retirement I needed something to do on 'foul weather' days.

First I found the author, A. Hyatt Verrill, from New Haven, Conn. He had been prolific and popular in his time but was forgotten, even to Wikipedia. His books were difficult to locate—they were acquired from used book dealers as far away as Australia and South Africa. They were such great reading I began to republish them. I started with an autobiography of the author, unpublished, that I located at University of British Columbia—that Archive had no idea how they acquired it!

So I entered the publishing business. I am using Lulu.Com; it is a print on demand publisher so the costs are quite manageable. I spent 15 years on Verrill!

Then I found 'Luke Allan', a Canadian, namely, Lacey Amy, who wrote stories while he travelled the world, but they were mostly about 'Blue Pete' an American half-breed who evades his enemies by going to Canada; Medicine Hat, Alberta, to be exact, and is befriended by a Mountie. Again these books were scarce, and no one knew this author was a Canadian. There are Stillwoods Editions of all of his 54 novels—two were originally published anonymously!

Lately, I've discovered New Brunswick's G. H. Teed, 1886-1938—prolific and forgotten. The vast majority of his 400+ novels were published anonymously and as 'pulp' novels. They were available weekly on England's newsstands and were very popular but as they were made of inferior paper, they deteriorated quickly. But over the years, English collectors speculated and researched these works, discovering the names of the individual authors, and G. H. Teed was one of the greatest!

Frank L. Packard was a famous writer in his day. Several of his novels were produced as major motion pictures. The Stillwoods

Edition books were created to fill in some of the holes— where modern versions were not available.

So that is the story on Stillwoods and myself, there are a few other authors and works I have added along in my journeys.

The quality of Stillwoods Editions is perhaps not great. I have no training in any of this digitizing and publishing business. I do not stop to make perfect products. I would rather have ten ones, than one ten!

I hope you enjoy these authors—their works are nearly a hundred years old!

Disclaimer: Each work may contain language and racial terms that is not appropriate to today. I apologize for them; I know that the author was using his voice to excite an adventurous audience. Most every work has characters of redeeming ethnicity within.

I hope you enjoy and share these stories; I have.

Doug Frizzle

frizzle@hfx.eastlink.ca

Stillwoods Editions of Frank Packard novels:
Broken Waters
Tiger Claws
Two Stolen Idols
The Iron Rider
Leigh, of the Royal North-West Mounted
Available at **http://www.lulu.com/spotlight/lulubook22**

BOOK I:

In the Underworld of Paris

CHAPTER I   AT TWELVE MINUTES PAST THREE

JOHN CRANE, known far and wide throughout the islands of Polynesia as one whose name was a synonym not merely for wealth but for a rugged integrity in his dealings with brown man and white alike, lay asleep aboard his ocean-going yacht in the Port of Havre, France. Suddenly he sat upright in bed. He was not only awake, but instantly alert. It was the habit of years—a great many of them; the training of a lifetime passed amidst surroundings where, as he was wont to say himself, a man had to learn to sleep awake if he wanted to awake alive.

Some one was knocking at his stateroom door. He reached out his hand with an irascible jerk, and pushed the button of the electric-light switch. Under a fringe of very heavy and shaggy grey eyebrows his blue eyes, sharp and steely, blinked for an instant in the flood of light. He glanced at his watch, which—another habit of his—always hung by its massive gold chain from the headpost of the brass bedstead when he was aboard.

It was twelve minutes past three in the morning.

The knocking was repeated.

Crane had a deep bass voice—a sea voice that had never been shackled. It racketed now through the cabin.

"I heard ye the first time," he roared. "Who's there?"

"It's Barlon, Mr. Crane, sir," a voice answered.

"Well, come in, blast ye!" Crane roared again.

The door opened, and a small, thin-faced man entered somewhat hesitantly. He was in decided dishabille. He had obviously pulled on a pair of trousers in haste, for his fingers were still nervously busy with various buttons; his bare feet were thrust into a pair of carpet slippers, and a steward's jacket, still unfastened, had been donned immediately over an undershirt—which latter, one might therefore perhaps be led to imagine, had done duty for night attire.

"Humph!" grunted Crane. "Now what the devil's the meaning of this? Some of the crew in a muss ashore, I suppose! Always are the night before sailing! Well, where's your tongue?"

"It's nothing to do with the crew, sir," Barlon answered. "It's a visitor for you."

Crane ran his fingers through a beard that, fiery red in spots, was beginning to speckle grey in others.

"A visitor!" he ejaculated. "And you knock me up for a visitor at twelve minutes past three in the morning!"

"I'm very sorry, sir," Barlon explained; "but it was the mate's orders—Mr. Miller's, sir. Mr. Miller said to tell you that a man has come aboard who says he must see you, sir—that it was a matter of very urgent importance. He was told that we were sailing at daylight, but he said it was all the more reason he must see you at once. And Mr. Miller says the man's not to be got rid of unless he's thrown ashore, and will he do that, sir, or will you see him?"

"What's his name?" demanded Crane.

"I can't say, sir." Barlon coughed suddenly, deprecatingly. "Mr. Miller says the man says you'd be better satisfied if no names were mentioned, sir."

Crane's eyes narrowed, but for a moment he made no reply. Judged by a past whose sixty-odd years had embraced at one time or another about every calling that a roving life in the tropics offered, the present situation was neither extraordinary nor unusual. Then, mentally, he shrugged his shoulders. John Crane had never refused himself to friend or enemy. It was perhaps a bit unconventional up here in France, but down in the islands —

"Well, bring him along!" ordered Crane curtly.

Barlon cocked his head jerkily to one side, as though he were uncertain that he had heard aright.

"Here, sir—in the stateroom?" he asked uneasily. "Did you say in here, sir?"

"I did!" said Crane caustically. "I'd light up the saloon and receive him there in state, only I'm not up on what's the correct thing to wear in these parts at this hour—and I'm not inspired by your example! Get out!"

The door closed hurriedly behind the little steward.

John Crane stared at the door panels for a moment meditatively, then he swung both feet out from under the covers and sat on the edge of the bed. He drew the pillow a little toward him so that, apparently, it quite inadvertently overlapped his hand. Beneath the pillow his fingers toyed with the butt of a revolver.

It was said of John Crane that he had never been caught napping.

He continued to stare at the door panels. He experienced now a sort of pleasurable curiosity in his prospective visitor. He was quite tired of civilization—a periodic condition with him—as periodic as in turn, some months later, he would tire and grow restless in his island home, and yearn for a cruise again and a temporary participation in the life of the great cities—London, Paris, New York—it mattered little which or where.

"I'm getting old," said John Crane suddenly to himself. "Always looking for a kick in my drink, and like the old drinker always finding it harder to get. Can't say I've got one out of this cruise. Maybe here's one—but I guess not. No such luck! Probably some down-and-outer that I borrowed a chew of tobacco from in Sarawak forty years ago, and who wants to get it back now at a trifling rate of interest, compounded of course."

Crane nodded his head vigorously.

"Yes," he said emphatically, "this meandering around ain't good enough. I'm getting too old for much more of it, and I'm glad the time has come to settle down a bit and *educate* that young nephew of mine, now that he's got his college degrees all framed! I guess I'll get a kick out of that. Lord, he must be twenty-four or five now—yes, twenty-five, for I've had him in that New York commission house for two years now. H'm! Maybe he's got a girl picked out; if he hasn't, I'll get him one—a real honest-to-God island girl that's got the morning sunrise in her eyes the way it comes up off old Talimi; and I guess an armchair on the verandah with a gin and tonic, watching the beggar running the plantation, and the kids running him and me too, ain't such a bad prospect in the offing. Let's see! I'll pick him up in New York in another eight days, and then we'll go down by the Canal to Fiji, and—"

John Crane became conscious that his fingers were toying with a revolver under the pillow.

"Well, I'm damned!" he ejaculated self-commiseratingly. "I guess I'm getting older than I thought I was!"

Footsteps sounded from the alleyway without. There was a knock again upon the door.

"Come in!" Crane's deep voice rumbled.

The door opened. A man stepped forward over the threshold and halted. Barlon, in the rear, stood with his hand on the doorknob as though awaiting orders.

Crane's blue eyes roved coolly over the stranger. The man still wore his hat, a soft-brimmed affair, and it was noticeably drawn well down over the eyes and forehead. From the man's shoulders hung a long black cloak of excellent texture, of the kind much affected by gentlemen on the continent for evening wear; the cloak hid both of the man's hands. Crane searched his memory. There was nothing in the slightest degree familiar about the stranger. The cloak seemed to bulge slightly under the man's left arm.

"Mr. Crane?" inquired the stranger.

The man's accent was plainly that of an Englishman.

"John Crane's my name," Crane answered, his eyes still searching the other critically.

"It's a beastly hour to force my way in upon you," the man said in a low voice. "I owe you an apology."

"The explanation of why you're here ought to take care of that," suggested Crane.

"Yes," said the man. "Quite so! Yes—of course!" He glanced over his shoulder significantly in the steward's direction. "Could we be alone?"

"Certain sure!" replied Crane promptly. "Barlon, close the door—on the other side!"

The door closed.

"Now?" invited Crane gruffly. "Perhaps we might start with your name? The introduction has been a bit one-sided so far. I do not recognize you —though if your hat were a little farther back I might perhaps have a better chance."

"My name is of no consequence, Mr. Crane," the other replied quietly. "However, it's Kendall." He threw his cloak back over his shoulders, disclosing the fact that he was in evening attire, and that the bulge under his left arm had obviously been caused by a large package wrapped in brown paper. He laid the package on the cabin settee, placed his hat beside it, and from his pocket took out a plain, sealed envelope which he handed to Crane. "My credentials," he said, with a faint smile.

Crane took the envelope and poised it in his hand while he again deliberately studied the man's face. The removal of the hat did not help any. He had never seen the other before in his life. He was quite sure of that; but he was equally sure he would never see the man again without recognizing him instantly. It was the clean shaven face of a man of perhaps forty; a rather pleasing face, resourcefulness in the firm lips, humour in the nest of wrinkles at the corners of the quiet grey eyes.

4

He tore the envelope open and—another habit of his—glanced first at the signature. The next instant, the revolver under the pillow utterly forgotten, he favoured his pyjama-covered knee with a mighty thump.

"From Martin Todd!" he exclaimed enthusiastically. "'Old Mouser,' we used to call him! Why in blazes didn't you say you came from Todd in the first place?"

Kendall's face broke into an expostulatory smile. "I think the letter will explain, Mr. Crane." Crane glanced at the letter. It bore neither date nor address.

"Where is he?" demanded Crane impetuously. "I haven't seen him in ten years."

"At present," said Kendall, "he's in Paris."

"Paris!" ejaculated Crane. "And I didn't know it! The last I heard of him he was in Russia."

"Yes," Kendall nodded. "So he was—all through the war, and, as I dare say you know, connected with the British Secret Service."

The steel had gone out of Crane's blue eyes; they were suddenly dreamy with a far-away look.

"Martin Todd in Paris—and me here in Havre!" he said. "The one man in the world I wouldn't miss seeing! We were pals for years together on the pearl beds. He fished me out from under the nose of a shark once—saved my life, by gad, in plain English, and nearly lost his own doing it. In Paris, eh? I was sailing at daybreak, but that's easily fixed. I ain't in any such hurry as that." Kendall shook his head quietly.

"The officer on deck informed me you were sailing then," he said; "and if you want to be of real assistance to Todd you won't make any change in your plans, Mr. Crane, or attempt to see him. The letter—" He paused with a suggestive smile.

"Humph!" grunted Crane; then, with a hoarse chuckle: "Yes, perhaps I *had* better read it."

The letter was on a single sheet of paper. Crane read it slowly, his brow puckering in a puzzled frown; then he re-read it, this time even more slowly and attentively than before:

Dear Crane:—

The friend of mine who presents this letter will make a rather strange request on my behalf. Obviously, as you will understand when he has talked to you, I cannot risk committing that request to paper. It will mean a whale of a lot, not only to me, but to many others, if you come through; but I don't want you to consider it for a minute just because we've been in a few tight holes together in the past if it's against your inclination and your better judgment. On that basis I would a hanged sight rather have you turn the proposition down flat; but I think it's just the sort of thing, with a touch of spice in it, that you'll be for strong—unless you've changed like the devil in the last ten years.

One word more—and it's only fair that I risk this much on paper: I am confident that my precautions have been such that there would be neither danger nor even inconvenience to you if you decided to 'sit in'; but, whichever way you decide, don't attempt to communicate with me—for both our sakes. During the last few days the stage has been reached where even my mail, I am convinced, is being tampered with.

Yours,
MARTIN TODD.

CHAPTER II   THE PACKAGE

JOHN CRANE laid the letter down, got out of bed and crossed the stateroom in his bare feet to the door. He opened the door suddenly and looked out; then, closing it again, he faced Kendall.

"If Martin Todd's in a mess," he said gruffly, "he's come to the right man. What does he want me to do?"

"To take care of that package for a little while," said Kendall, indicating the brown paper parcel on the settee.

"Take care of that package?" repeated Crane. "What is it?"

"I'll show you," replied Kendall briefly.

He picked up the package, rapidly untied the heavy string with which it was fastened, removed the wrapping paper, and laid the contents out on the settee.

"Good Lord A'mighty!" gasped John Crane suddenly.

He stared, blinking, at what was before him on the settee. His jaw was slightly dropped. He fingered his tawny beard a little helplessly, glanced at Kendall as though to reassure himself that the man was there in flesh and blood, that the whole thing was not an attack of hallucination, and then his eyes fastened on the settee again. On a bed of snowy cotton wadding, accentuating their brilliancy and lustre, lay a magnificent assortment of jewels and ornaments embracing, it seemed to him, every precious stone he had ever heard of. They were there in the form of tiaras, pendants, bracelets, rings, earrings—all in exquisite settings; also there was a pearl necklace which, if genuine, he appraised instantly as alone being worth a fortune.

John Crane *knew* pearls. He leaned forward, took up the necklace and examined it critically.

"My word!" He whistled softly under his breath, "Yes, it's the real thing, right enough!"

Kendall laughed.

"Of course, it is!" he said. "It belongs to the Princess Ludov. But here's the complete list." He picked up a slip of paper that had been wrapped with the jewels, and handed it to Crane.

Crane studied the paper, knitting his brows. It contained a list of seven Russian names; and opposite each name was indicated one or more of the jewels which, presumably, comprised the assortment on the settee.

Crane returned the necklace to its original resting place on the cotton wadding, and laid the slip of paper down beside it. He fumbled for a pocket and a cigar. Discovering that he was in pyjamas, he procured a box of Manillas from a stand of drawers, offered one to Kendall, bit off the end of another and lighted it. He sat down on the edge of the bed.

"I won't say you haven't given me a bit of a shock," he said, "because you have. I'm beginning to get a dim idea of what it's all about from that list—but you go ahead, Mr. Kendall, and spin the yarn."

"It won't take long," Kendall answered. "It's simple enough, and there's no mystery about it. You know what's been happening in Russia lately, and you know Martin Todd too well to make it necessary for me to tell you he's the kind of man that's pretty loyal to his friends. He's been in Russia until a few months ago. As I said, you know what's been going on there. Any of the nobility that got off with their lives, got off lucky— the confiscation of estates, property and personal belongings was merely the daily routine and the commonplace. Those that weren't trapped in the first place became fugitives, and in many cases absolutely destitute. They're scattered all over the world."

"I've run across one or two myself," said Crane, a sudden quiet in his voice.

"Yes," said Kendall. "Well, those jewels there belong to that little group of people whose names you have just read, and who, in the many years he was in Russia, had come to form Todd's circle of intimates. Those jewels are all they saved—and Todd saved them. Owing to his being an Englishman, and in a sense in an official position, he managed to get out of the country with what you see there. The details would take until daylight to tell. So far, four out of the seven on that list have reached Paris. The others haven't been heard of yet. They were all to rendezvous in Paris, you understand. And now, here's the crux of the whole matter. How, I don't know; but the Soviet agents know about these jewels. Every one of the four I have mentioned is being watched, and so is Todd himself. The jewels can't be sold here, they can't be turned into money—the main thing for the moment is to get them secretly out of the country to some other place where, later, they can be disposed of for the benefit of their owners."

Crane nodded his head.

"I've known Martin Todd intimately," Kendall went on, "perhaps not so long as you have, but for a good many years. I've a little bachelor apartment in Paris, and it has always been Todd's habit to stay with me on his frequent visits there. That's how I appear in the matter. In a way, I am under surveillance too; but not quite to the same extent as Todd and the others. We talked first of my taking the jewels and making a dash for it, but we gave up the idea almost at once because, obviously, since Todd was known to be living with me, any prolonged absense on my part would only transfer the particular attention of the Soviet agents to myself. The jewels were well hidden, we weren't afraid that they were in any imminent danger of being discovered, but the situation was becoming more and more unbearable and dangerous to all concerned; and, for all the good they were, those jewels might as well have been so many pebbles. Our problem was to find some one who was not only willing and in a position to help us, but some one in whom, at the same time, *we* could put absolute trust. We were at our wits' ends, when Todd saw in the paper that your yacht was here at Havre. He was like a kid in his excitement. 'If Crane will do it, and I think he will,' he said, 'the whole Russian nation couldn't get them away from the old beggar again.'"

Crane indulged in a throaty chuckle.

"A nation's a bit more than I ever took on before, though I've stood off a native tribe or so," he said. "But that sounds like Todd. Well, go on."

"That's about all," said Kendall. "It was only necessary to draw attention away from me for a few hours. Early this morning Todd, accompanied by the four refugees, led the agents on a wild-goose chase to the outskirts of Paris. Meanwhile, I attended a somewhat formal dinner at a friend's house to which I had been invited, and at which a large number of guests were present. It was, as a matter of fact, quite a social event, and therefore entirely removed from any possible connection with this affair. After dinner there were cards and dancing; and during the course of the evening I slipped out into the garden unobserved, climbed a fence or two, and gained a side street several blocks away. I did not risk going near my own motor, of course; so I rented one from a garage in another part of the city—and here I am."

Crane's blue eyes snapped approval.

"Good work!" he grunted. "So you motored from Paris? You made some time."

"I did," said Kendall grimly. "And I've got to make it in just as good time going back. I want to be seen in my usual haunts by breakfast hour." He looked inquiringly at Crane for an instant. "Well, that's the whole story. What do you say, Mr. Crane? Will you sail off with these, or shall I sail back with them to Paris?"

"Why, I've already said, haven't I?" said John Crane, elevating his shaggy eyebrows in surprise. "Certain sure, I'll take 'em! Yes, and"—he thumped his knee emphatically again—"I'd take 'em under the circumstances, by glory, even if Martin Todd hadn't anything to do with 'em! And now let's set down to cases. You haven't got any time to spare. What am I to do with 'em, except keep 'em?"

"Nothing," replied Kendall. "As I understand from Todd, you live on an island somewhere in the South Seas—and the paper said you were returning there."

"Yes," said Crane. "Talimi's the name of it."

Kendall nodded.

"Well, nobody'll look for these jewels on an island in the South Seas, that's certain. Todd wants you to keep them there until things clear up here, and it's safe for some one to go for them."

"H'm!" said Crane judicially. "It's a long way to come."

"Yes," Kendall agreed; "but it's not so far from Sydney, or Auckland, or some other centre down there where they could be disposed of with no chance of trouble, such as there would be anywhere in Europe, or probably, for that matter, in America."

"Yes; that's so," admitted Crane. "But what about my handing them over when the time comes? It's got to be either to you or Martin Todd in person—is that the idea?"

Kendall shook his head.

"No; it wouldn't do to make it so hard and fast as that," he said. "Todd and I talked that point over. We might not either of us be able to go—indeed, it's not likely we would. That would tie the thing up completely. It's more than probable that when you eventually hand the jewels over it will be to one or more of the actual owners whose names are on that list there."

"But I don't know them," objected Crane; "and I can't be responsible for their identification. What about that?"

Kendall smiled.

"You can give Todd credit for this—it's simple and effective. Have you got a pen here, Mr. Crane, and a piece of paper?"

"Sure," said John Crane, jerking his head in the direction of a portable writing case on top of the stand of drawers.

"All right," said Kendall. "Then just copy that list of names and jewels, keep the original yourself, and give the copy to me. That copy, in your own handwriting, which, however cleverly it might be attempted, could hardly be duplicated without you detecting it, will identify whoever presents it as the one to whom you are to deliver the jewels."

Crane pursed his lips.

"Yes, that's good enough—damned good, in fact; but suppose it's stolen from you in the meantime— or lost?"

"It won't be stolen," said Kendall quietly; "but granted that it is, what could the thief do with it? It's absolutely meaningless so far as John Crane and the Island of Talimi are concerned, isn't it? As for being lost, that, though unlikely, is of course quite another matter. In that case there would be nothing for it but that Todd or myself would have to go to you in person."

"Right, you are!" said Crane with a whimsical smile. "I haven't got anything more to say! I guess you and Martin Todd haven't overlooked any bets." He got up, secured the writing case, and returned to the bed. "Let's have that list," he said.

Thereafter for the space of several minutes there was no sound in the cabin save the scratching of John Crane's pen; then he looked up and handed the slip of paper on which he had been writing, together with the original list, to Kendall.

"There you are," he said.

Kendall compared the two papers carefully, folded and placed the copy in his pocket, and remained with the original in his hand.

"We've only to check this now with the jewels there," he said, "and I'm off."

"Have we got to do that?" grunted Crane. "Todd's word is good enough for me."

"Yes, I know; but I'd very much prefer that we should, just the same, for your sake," said Kendall earnestly. "It won't take but a moment, and it precludes the possibility of any misunderstanding arising as to the exact contents of the package when you received it."

"Fire ahead, then," said Crane.

He got up once more and moved over to the settee.

The two men checked the list with the contents of the package and found them to correspond.

Kendall wrapped the jewels up again, tied the package, and handed it, together with the original list, to Crane.

"I'll say good-bye now, Mr. Crane," he said with grave smile. "I'm not going to thank you, but you can be sure that you'll never turn into your bed any night after this without more than one fervent blessing being called down upon your head."

"Well," said Crane dryly, "there are some people I know of that would say I need a blessing or two!" He placed the package and list in one of the drawers of the stand. "I'll see that these are put safely away in the morning. Is there anything you'd like before you go—a nip of something?"

"No," said Kendall; "thanks all the same. I'm better without it in view of the trip I've got ahead of me."

"Right!" said Crane. "It's a bit chilly for my tropical bones on deck in this attire, or I'd see you off." He pushed the bell-button—and held out his hand. "Tell Martin Todd that old John Crane ain't changed any, and that Talimi ain't a bad place to visit. Savvy? Good luck to you!"

"I'll tell him," said Kendall heartily. He lowered his voice as a step sounded in the alleyway. "I would suggest that my name is Howard."

"Right!" said Crane again; and then, as Barlon appeared in the doorway: "I'll think it over, Mr. Howard, and let you know from New York. Barlon, see that Mr. Howard gets ashore all right."

"Thank you, Mr. Crane," said Kendall. "Goodnight, sir."

The door closed.

John Crane returned to his bed and extinguished his light. But it was a long time before he got to sleep. It was possibly on that account he arose much later than was his usual custom that morning.

When he went on deck it was to find that the yacht had been under way for several hours—and that the wireless was out of order.

CHAPTER III   L'Ange Du Quartier

IT was not a nice quarter of Paris, nor was the night—the one that followed John Crane's departure from Havre—a nice one in any particular. There was an intermittent drizzle, and the street lights showed merely as curiously suspended globules through the blanket of greyish mist that lay upon the city. Here and there a yellow glow was discernible from a lighted window or perchance from a doorway, but these were few and far between. It was a locality very prone to closed shutters.

The fiacre was archaic, a ramshackle affair that creaked in every joint and made complaint at every inequality in the road; the horse was old and unenthusiastic; the *cocher* who drove the vehicle was down at the heels in appearance, slovenly clothed and coarse of feature.

Anne Walton, a slim and dainty figure, quietly but very trimly dressed, stared out from right to left with wide brown eyes as she bumped along. Beside her on the seat lay a well-filled basket or hamper. For the first time on one of these excursions, that had earned for her the title of *L'Ange du Quartier,* she was a little ill at ease, a little disturbed. The Paris underworld—at least that section of it which she knew and frequented—held no terrors for her; on that score she felt that she was quite safe. She did not tell tales; she never sought to probe into matters that were no concern of hers; nor did she ever attempt to satisfy even a moderate curiosity.

There was a distinct line of demarcation between crime, however sordid it might be, and stark, hopeless distress; though the latter might be, and often was, but the corollary of the first—and she had learned to ask no questions. It was not, therefore, her present surroundings that disturbed her—it was the *cocher* on the box of her fiacre. He had a villainous cast of countenance. But she had had no choice. He had, as it were, been forced upon her. It was a night when vehicles of all descriptions were at once in demand, and on emerging from her apartment, a rather fashionable one in rather a fashionable street, the concierge had been able to find no other conveyance for her.

Her father (Anne did not remember her mother) undoubtedly would not have approved, quite probably would not have permitted it had he been at home, but he had gone away that morning on business for a few days as he frequently did. But then her father had never approved of this work of hers amongst the slums. On the other hand, he had never actually forbidden it. Ordinarily she did not make these visits at night, but circumstances had prevented her from visiting Madame Frigon either that day or the day before, and she was a little worried about Madame Frigon. Madame Frigon was grievously poor, and had a serious valvular affection of the heart which was in no way ameliorated by the old woman's alcoholic propensities—propensities which had of late been alarmingly on the increase.

Anne shook her head. She could not understand where or how Madame Frigon procured her stock of liquor. There was, to a certainty, not a crust of bread at the present moment in Madame Frigon's rat-haunted attic (Madame Frigon called it her apartment) under the eaves of one of the most wretched edifices in Paris, but with equal certainty there was a bottle or two of the most fiery liquid to be found anywhere in the city hidden there. The end was inevitable, of course—some day Madame Frigon would die in her cups, climaxing her sordid life with a wholly miserable death. It was a pitiable case. Madame Frigon from girlhood, and especially *in* her girlhood, had been everything that was unmentionable; she was not unacquainted with the police, nor the police with her—but the police did not worry about her any more. To-day she was too old to give trouble, a semi-invalid scarcely able to get about—an ancient bit of driftwood waterlogged near to the sinking point. Anne had first heard of Madame Frigon from some of the other "cases" on her list. She had sought the old woman out, found her in literally a starving condition, and since then had provided for her. Hence the basket on the seat of the fiacre.

Anne's thoughts reverted to the *cocher* on the box. She remembered the look on the man's face when she had given him the address to which he was to take her— she was afraid it had been almost a leer. It was not incomprehensible. He was of that type. A young lady from a fashionable apartment, unaccompanied, who desired to be taken to one of the city's most unsavoury localities at night, might very easily suggest a rendezvous to a mind not above such deductions—and a rendezvous to the possessor of such a mind might very easily suggest fair game in one way or another. Certainly the man's tongue had been in his cheek.

Perhaps, though, she was doing the poor cabman an injustice. He had been civil enough; and, at least, he was not taking her out of her way, for she had recognized several landmarks as she drove along. In any case, in the open streets of Paris, even in a fog, there should be little need for concern; and, anyway, she was quite capable of taking care of herself, at least she always had been, even in tight corners—and to one brought up as she had been in the open, and sometimes uncivilized spaces of the South Seas, tight corners had not been unknown to her.

Anne pursed her lips suddenly. Half of the year she and her father spent in Paris, and half in those same South Seas on the Island of Talimi, where her father had a plantation; and yesterday her father had announced that in another month their Paris "season" would be over and they would be returning to Talimi. She was not quite sure whether she was pleased or sorry. She loved Talimi with its freedom and its tropical beauty, its soft perfumed breezes and its warmth and colour; but, also, she loved Paris. She had an intimate circle of friends here, she lived a very wonderful and happy social life, and she was intensely interested in this self-imposed work of hers amongst what might almost be called the pariahs and outcasts of even the poor. Still, she was never sure whether she was glad or sorry when, in turn, she left Talimi for Paris, or Paris for Talimi. She was happy in both places. She smiled a little to herself. Why consider the matter? Surely she had alternated between the two places often enough to have become philosophical about it!

The fiacre stopped. Anne looked out. It was very dark, and, save for the two small lamps of the fiacre, which were but sputters of yellow in the murk, there was no light at all. She could, however, distinguish the outlines of the building that faced her across the sidewalk—an almost disintegrated three-story frame house with a peaked roof that slanted at acute angles. It was Madame Frigon's. Madame Frigon lived in the garret under the peaked roof.

Anne took her basket and stepped out. The *cocher* had got down from his box. He did not offer to help her with the basket; he merely stood quite close to her, his head thrust forward a little, staring at her. Anne stopped suddenly. One of the fiacre's lamp threw the man's face into half-relief. His smile now was most distinctly a leer, and there was an ugly glitter in his eyes as they fastened on the purse in her hand. Anne's heart beat a little faster—perhaps the man did not realize that the light from the fiacre's lamp, poor as it was, was on his face. There was no mistaking his intention now—or his viciousness.

She selected a coin from her purse and offered it to the other.

The man's hand reached out quickly, not so much, it seemed to Anne, in the direction of the coin as in the direction of the purse—and as suddenly drew back, while he shook his head, and his lips expanded into what obviously was intended for a reassuring grin.

Footsteps, approaching, had sounded on the pavement.

"But, no, mademoiselle," expostulated the *cocher,* "there is no hurry—eh?—'ere nom! There will be time enough for mademoiselle to pay when I have taken her back."

Anne smiled a little grimly now. The footsteps were rapidly coming nearer, and they were very comforting.

"I shall not need you any more," said Anne quietly. "There is your money."

"But mademoiselle will find no other fiacre on such a night in this *quartier,"* protested the man smoothly. "It is impossible that mademoiselle should walk home. Mademoiselle will perhaps not be long; but, even if she is, what does it matter? She will pay me well, I am sure. I will wait for her."

The footsteps had come up almost abreast of the fiacre now, and a man's form bulked in queer, grotesque outlines through the mist. In another moment the footsteps would be retreating, and she would be left alone again. It was quite true what the *cocher* said, that she would almost certainly find no other means of conveyance for her return journey; but that was very much the lesser of the two evils. To step into the fiacre of this gargoylefaced brute again was to return home certainly minus her purse—if she returned home at all.

"You will do nothing of the sort!" Anne said sharply. "There is your fare!"

She tossed the coin onto the seat of the fiacre, and, carrying her basket, darted across the sidewalk, opened the door of the house, ran inside, and closed the door after her. It was intensely dark here and she could not see a foot in front of her, but she knew the way, and, not at all sure but that the *cocher* would attempt to follow her, she made no pause. Still running, she began to mount the stairs.

The staircase was old, dilapidated and shaky, and, in her haste, the treads creaked hideously, shattering the silence of the house with appalling noises. From behind a door, somewhere on the first landing, a voice, heavy either with sleep or drink, cursed her with profane abandon for the din she made. After that she went more slowly, feeling her way— the street door she was quite sure had not opened behind her.

From the third landing, a few steps, more like a ladder than a flight of stairs, led upward to Madame Frigon's domain. Anne mounted these and rapped at the door that confronted her. At first there was no response, and Anne rapped again. There came then a sudden co-mingled sound of grumbling and creaking from within; and then a voice, hoarse, raucous and unsteady, but marvellously fluent with uncomplimentary epithets, invited the unprintable cause of the disturbance to betake itself to an unprintable destination of which hell was merely a suburb.

"Madame Frigon, open the door!" said Anne severely. "It is Mademoiselle Walton."

The voice dropped instantly into a soft and almost crooning note; the creaking, evidently from a cot or bed of some kind, was renewed with greater violence, as though some one were rising in haste, and a step came shuffling across the floor.

The door was flung open. It was as dark within as it was without. Anne could see nothing.

"Tiens!" cried the voice. "So it is *la petite ange,* eh? Well, come in! Come in, mademoiselle!" Anne stepped through the doorway.

"Could we not have a little light, Madame Frigon?" she inquired pleasantly.

"But yes, mademoiselle! Instantly!" replied Madame Frigon. "Instantly!"

Madame Frigon's "instantly" was of some duration. There was more shuffling of feet, first in one direction and then in another, and something overturned with a crash on the floor. Madame Frigon began to snarl viciously again:

"Sacré nom! . . . Les allumettes . . . Le diable s'en mêle . . ."

Anne waited patiently. In the first place Madame Frigon was lame, and in the second place Anne was not without suspicion that Madame Frigon had had very recent recourse to a bottle. Finally a match flame spurted up through the darkness, and then a candlewick, diffidently at first, gave forth a flickering, yellow and inadequate light.

"Voilà!" exclaimed Madame Frigon triumphantly.

Anne set down her basket. The attic was in utter disorder, painfully bare, and none too clean. The candle was stuck in the neck of a bottle, and the bottle stood on a rickety chair beside a cot, which, due to a splintered leg, sagged perilously at one corner. The covering of the cot was an old blanket that was torn and full of holes. The only other article in sight was the chair, quite as rickety as its fellow, that Madame Frigon had already upset on the floor. Madame Frigon, herself, was in keeping with her surroundings. She was ageless. She might have been sixty—or ninety. Her hair was that indefinite shade between grey and white. Her eyes were black; and once, when her face had been less like a mask of wrinkled parchment, and there had been colour in her cheeks, and her skin had been soft and smooth (incredible!) those eyes must have been very beautiful and effective. Her dress was a wrapper, a flaming calico thing, that gaped immodestly at the breast.

Madame Frigon limped to the overturned chair and righted it.

"Sit down, my dear, sit down!" she invited heartily. Her eyes were on Anne's basket.

"Did you think I had forgotten you, Madame Frigon?" Anne smiled. "I was terribly sorry that I could not get here yesterday—and all to-day it was impossible."

"And to-night," said Madame Frigon reprovingly, "you should not have come, either. *Bon Dieu,* I would have done very well until to-morrow! It is a bad night, and even on a good one this is no neighbourhood for such as you."

"Nonsense!" said Anne brightly. "I am not afraid of anybody in this neighbourhood—unless it is the *cocher* who brought me here, who is not of this neighbourhood at all, and whom I have sent away."

"The *cocher!"* Madame Frigon made a grimace. "You are right. I do not like a *cocher* myself. The last one that drove me—I do not remember when it was—robbed me of three sous. *Pardieu!* And this one, mademoiselle—what did he do?"

"Well," said Anne, and laughed lightly now, "if some one had not very fortunately come along the street at the moment, I am afraid he would have robbed me of my purse."

"Le miserable!" exclaimed Madame Frigon indignantly. "What did I say? They are all alike. And so you sent him away?"

"Of course," said Anne.

Madame Frigon shook her head with sudden owl-like gravity.

"C'est bien drole, ca! I was not asleep, though I did not answer mademoiselle at once, for one has a care as to who is outside the

18

door—eh?—and I did not expect mademoiselle. And I heard a horse stop down there—but I did not hear it go away. *Tiens!* We will see, *ma petite!"*

Madame Frigon hobbled over to the window, flung open the shutters, and, leaning out, peered down into the street. She began to mutter something under her breath, and then suddenly she raised her voice.

"Get out of there!" she screamed. "Get out you —you—*maudit* son of a sewer rat!"

A voice floated up from below in retort wholly as uncomplimentary, and with added injunctions to the old woman to mind her own business and keep her mouth shut. Madame Frigon drew in her head and hobbled back to the cot.

"He is still there, *le saligaud!"* shrilled Madame Frigon. "But have no fear, mademoiselle. He will not be there long, though he will have reason to remember Madame Frigon for a long time!" She clawed under the mattress of her cot, produced a bottle, uncorked it, and placed it to her lips.

"Madame Frigon!" expostulated Anne sharply.

"Bah!" said Madame Frigon. "There is but a drop in it, it is true—but would you have me waste good liquor on a *vaurien* like that! *Tiens!* You will see!" She emptied the bottle at a gulp, and once more shuffled across the floor to the window.

"What are you going to do, Madame Frigon?" demanded Anne still more sharply.

Madame Frigon was in the midst of a tirade directed at the *cocher* on the sidewalk; she paused to cackle with malicious glee over her shoulder at Anne.

"I am going to teach him manners, *ce p'tit bon-homme, la!"*

An opprobrious flood of language drifted up from the sidewalk.

"Mon Dieu!" screamed back Madame Frigon. "But your throat must be dry after all that—eh? Here is a bottle for you—open your mouth wide!"

Madame Frigon hurled the bottle with all her strength.

A wild howl and a crash of splintering glass rewarded her effort. A window below opened; another opened in the adjoining house— and the *cocher* became the target of more maledictions and still another bottle. It was not a nice neighbourhood. The *cocher* drove off; his horse, judging from the rapidity of the hoof beats, enthusiastic for once.

The fracas subsided. Madame Frigon drew in her head from the window and closed the shutters.

"You see!" said she proudly. "It is true that, because it was dark, I missed his head, but I did not miss *him!*"

Anne shook her head.

"You might have injured him badly," she said severely.

Madame Frigon sat down on the edge of her cot again.

"And why not?" she inquired. "Everybody would be better off, including himself. But anyway he is gone. And now what is mademoiselle going to do? How is she going to return home?"

"Oh, don't worry about that, Madame Frigon," said Anne, lightly. "I shouldn't have gone with him anyway; and since I shall have no basket to carry on the way back, I don't in the least mind walking until I get to where I can find a bus, or a cab, or a taxi, or something. I told you before that I felt quite safe on the streets anywhere around here."

"No one is safe on the streets around here at night," declared Madame Frigon sententiously. "And a young girl like you with those eyes, and those lips—*quelle adorable figure!*—bah!—safe! No one is safe here. In the daytime perhaps, yes. But at night—no. And especially in the last few days. Have you not heard?" She lowered her voice, and glanced furtively around the shadowy, candle-lighted attic. "It is said that Fire-Eyes and his *canaille* have their rendezvous here now; anyway, there is more than one who swears he has seen Fire-Eyes."

"Fire-Eyes?" said Anne, not over-much impressed. "That is an English name."

"*C'est possible!*" Madame Frigon shrugged her shoulders. "How should I know? Some say he is English, some say he is an Italian, or a Spaniard, or something else. The devil, who alone is his master, knows what he is. What does it matter? It is enough that he is Fire-Eyes. That is his name."

"But who is this Fire-Eyes, and what does he do?" asked Anne.

Madame Frigon's jaw sagged a little helplessly as she gazed at Anne.

"*Mon Dieu!*" she whispered. "Mademoiselle asks who is Fire-Eyes? *C'est incroyable!* You are going to tell me that you have never heard of Fire-Eyes?"

Anne nodded her head.

"I am afraid I never did," she admitted.

"Listen, then!" said Madame Frigon. "I will tell you!" Again she glanced furtively around the attic. "They say he has powers that are given to him by the devil"—she crossed herself hurriedly— "that he hears everything; that he knows everything. And I believe it—*nom de Dieu,* why should I not believe it? I have seen it with my own eyes. But they are wrong about him, and I was wrong when I said the devil alone is his master—it is the other way around. *Sucre nom,* I, Madame Frigon, tell you, it is the other way around—it is he who is either the devil himself, or the devil's master. He makes one do things with his eyes. They burn— like—like skewers that are made red-hot and are stuck into you; and they read what is in your soul, those eyes. You do not understand—you have never seen him with that cloak wrapped around his shoulders, and just the eyes showing between the black beard and the rim of the round black hat, that is like the hat that sometimes the priests wear. Only once have I seen him—but I have not forgotten. One never forgets. And it was ten years ago. It was in a place where one like mademoiselle would never be. Listen!" Madame Frigon reached out a hand that trembled, and grasped convulsively at Anne's arm. "I saw him kill a girl there—and for nothing at all. In a moment of anger—and yet he was like one who was doing no more than if he was lighting a cigarette. And I was close— as close as I am to mademoiselle now. And he was smiling, and he had a knife, a long, ugly thing in his hand, and he leaned toward her and—"

Madame Frigon suddenly jerked back her hand, and, with a shudder, covered her eyes—"I cannot tell it! *Nom de Dieu de Dieu,* I cannot tell it! I ran screaming into the street. And I have been afraid ever since, for he never forgets, and if he ever saw me again he would remember me and he would kill me as he killed *la pauvre Tisotte,* for I would be a witness against him."

Anne's eyes were wide, her face a little white.

"That is horrible," she said in a low voice. "You mean that the man has earned a reputation for wanton murder, and trades on the fear that he inspires as a human butcher at large? I think I understand."

"No," said Madame Frigon; "he is much more than that. He is"— there was awe in Madame Frigon's face now, and, mingling with the awe, a curious note of admiration—"he is a great criminal. *Un maître!* And he has his followers—*le bon Dieu* knows how many—but they spring up everywhere—they are his eyes and his ears—but he has the brains."

"But the police!" exclaimed Anne. "If he is known to have committed so many crimes, why do not the police get him?"

"The police! Bah!" Madame Frigon cackled suddenly, shrilly. "It would take more than the police! Have I not told you he is of the devil? How else will mademoiselle explain it? More than once they have trapped Fire-Eyes. He is inside the house. The house is surrounded entirely, you understand? There is no escape. And then the *agents,* from the front and the back and the roof and the cellar, rush in, and—poof!—Fire-Eyes is not there. Then for months Fire-Eyes does not exist. He has disappeared. Nowhere is he heard of. He is dead. Like that, mademoiselle—dead. And then, *tout d'un coup,* under the very noses of the police, Fire-Eyes has snatched a new little bouquet for himself out of some rich man's garden and is off again with thousands of francs in his pocket, and, more than likely, leaving another murder behind him."

"I see!" said Anne, with a grim little *moue.* "He is not a nice person, and I hope I shall not meet him. But I hardly think I shall. From what you say, he is too important to be a Mère footpad, and so, in spite of your Monsieur Fire-Eyes, I am quite sure I shall be perfectly safe on the way back. But, anyway, do not let us talk about it any more. See, here is a basket for you, and—"

"Yes!" Madame Frigon nodded her head vigorously, a little eagerly. She stretched out her hand for the basket. "Yes, it is good of mademoiselle, so good! I do not want to talk about the *maudit* any more, either. It is to give one the shivers! *Tiens! Tiens! Tiens!* But mademoiselle is *une ange!* I pray for mademoiselle every night— every night, you understand? *Bon Dieu,* I do not know what I would do but for mademoiselle."

Anne smiled and patted the old hag on the shoulder reassuringly.

"Don't worry about that, Madame Frigon," she said; "though, as a matter of fact, you will very soon have to do without me for a while, for I am going away in another month. I will arrange, though, that you will be looked after while I am gone."

"You are going away!" Madame Frigon stared aghast. Her wrinkled face assumed a forlorn and helpless look. *"Oh, bon Dieu!"*

"But I will come back," said Anne, and laughed the old woman's very evident distress away.

She explained her visit to her island home in Talimi, told Madame Frigon of the life there; and, from that, drifted to the subject of Madame Frigon herself. Anne proved a very magisterial young lady, and quite severe. Madame Frigon was to leave the bottle alone. Did Madame Frigon not realize that it was doing her infinite harm? Surely Madame Frigon was old enough to understand— it was not as though she were a child. How could Madame Frigon expect to get better when she would not obey the doctor that she, Anne, sent her?

And much more. . . .

Madame Frigon was more than usually penitent. It was finished forever—*la boisson!* She would never touch a drink again!

At the end of half an hour Anne took her leave.

Madame Frigon limped to the door, holding the candle which had almost burned out.

"If it were not for this leg—this cursed leg," said Madame Frigon bitterly, "I would go with you. I do not like it, mademoiselle. It is a bad night. It is not for a child like you to be out alone."

"Oh, dear!" said Anne, and smiled teasingly. "Are we going over all that again? Everybody knows me around here, and it is absurd to give it another thought. Good-night, Madame Frigon, and remember all I have said—and especially about the doctor. He was very angry the last time I saw him."

"Yes, yes!" said Madame Frigon hastily. "Yes —*oh, bon Dieu,* yes!—I will remember! He shall have no reason to complain again. If he does, mademoiselle—listen!—he will be telling lies. Good-night, mademoiselle, and the blessing of the Sainted Mother rest upon you!"

"Good-night again," said Anne, and made her way, quietly and without noise this time, down the three rickety flights of stairs in the darkness, and, opening the front door, stepped out on the street.

CHAPTER IV   IN THE ALLEYWAY

THE mist, if anything, seemed to have grown heavier. Anne paused outside the door and peered about her; she did not quite know why she did this, save that it was done instinctively and, perhaps, though she had heard the fiacre drive away, to reassure herself that the man had really gone. The curb was empty, and, so far as she could see, the sidewalk in both directions was deserted. Nor was there any sound. A sense of loneliness suddenly took possession of her; the silence seemed unnatural, even uncanny. It was not like Paris to be silent, and especially this particular *quartier,* where brawls were too common to attract even passing attention. What a beastly night it was anyway! She would have quite a long way to go before she could find a conveyance of any sort—she had been very blithe about that a few minutes ago!— quite a long way through blocks of narrow, squalid streets that, in turn, were intersected by a network of darker lanes and alleyways still less inviting.

"Stupid!" said Anne suddenly and very scornfully to herself. "You are letting Madame Frigon's tales frighten you. Now please don't be absurd!"

She set off resolutely along the street; but, nevertheless, for all the austere little smile on her lips, her scorn at her childishness, and her quick, easy, reliant stride, she was, inwardly, not at all at her ease. It was all very well, but it wasn't pleasant; and she had imagination, and the darkness and the queer silence, seemed somehow to prod that imagination into conjuring up all manner of fancies. She wished that Madame Frigon had not been quite so realistic about that girl Tisotte and that brutal fiend with the grotesque name of Fire-Eyes. Otherwise, she wouldn't have thought anything at all about this little walk; whereas now she couldn't think about anything else, and was, every other moment or so, possessed of a panicky impulse to run at the top of her speed.

"I am positively ashamed of you!" said Anne to herself indignantly. "I never knew you were such a little coward!"

Anne walked rapidly on for several blocks, meeting no one, hearing no sound save that of her own footsteps, until, about to turn a corner, she came abruptly to a halt. The silence was suddenly and rudely broken. From somewhere—she could not place the direction, for the sound seemed to be confused with its own echoes—a shot rang out. Then another, and another, and then a crackle of spasmodic firing. There was shouting too—hoarse, angry yells—then a shot again. The sounds seemed to be close at hand, and yet, too, they seemed to be curiously muffled as though at some distance away. It was perhaps the acoustic properties of the night—the fog blanket, that confused the sense of hearing as well as the sense of sight. And for a moment Anne stood irresolute. She was not at all sure now but that she infinitely preferred the silence with its depressing sense of isolation. Well, here was the silence again, then! The sounds died away—there was utter stillness once more. It was so strange! No windows had been opened, no heads inquisitively thrust out, as in the case of the fiacre driver outside Madame Frigon's attic. The neighbourhood, when it came to anything that might involve really serious consequences, was obviously apathetic, callously so—on the principle, no doubt, that it was no affair of anybody's save those engaged in the exchange of their own unholy pleasantries. A none too gentle school of experience, perhaps, had long since taught the *quartier* the imprudence of enacting the role of "innocent bystander."

Anne went on again, but even more rapidly now than before. She was conscious now that her spirited and self-inflicted tongue lashings were hopelessly ineffective; she was, as she expressed it to herself, a bit "jumpy," and she simply could not help it. She was not afraid in the sense that terror in any way possessed her; she would have died rather than behave like a coward, though she had already called herself one—but she very heartily wished herself at the present moment anywhere but where she was.

Her way lay around the next corner. Anne turned this—and, a quarter way along the block, halted again as abruptly as before. There was no mistaking the direction from which the sounds came now that she heard again, and which, with the exception of the shots, had suddenly broken out anew. There were shouts, and the pound of racing feet— many of them, heavy-booted feet, making a loud clatter on the sidewalk—and they were coming toward her along the sidewalk at a furious pace. She could not see any one. Twenty yards away the mist was impenetrable. She drew quickly in against the wall of the house beside which she had halted; and then, discovering that the house made the corner of a lane just a yard or so ahead of her, she darted forward, and, slipping into the lane, crouched there motionless.

The sounds of the pounding feet came nearer and nearer; shapes, strangely formless in the mist, began to flit past the mouth of the lane; oaths, snarls, vicious exclamations reached her; she heard the deep, hard, gasping breaths from straining lungs. It was as though a savage pack of beasts was hot on the trail and merciless in the pursuit of some quarry. She had tried to count the flitting shapes —but they were mostly a confused blur. There must, however, have been at least six or seven of them—she was sure of that. It was strange, though, that the "quarry" had not passed her before she came into the lane here, since she had come from the direction in which they were now running. Perhaps, though, they had almost closed with their "quarry;" that he, or she, or whatever it was, was merely leading by a bare yard or so, and was, perhaps, but the first of those shapes that had swept by in the mist. But if so they had not yet brought their prey to earth, for she could still hear the pound of feet, receding and more faintly now, it was true, but quite as quick in tempo as before.

A few seconds passed—perhaps ten, perhaps thirty of them, perhaps more. To Anne it seemed a time interminable as she crouched there listening, and then the last sound died away in the distance. Anne straightened up, discovered that her small fists were tightly clenched, and that her heart was thumping with unpleasant rapidity. She was not at all pleased with herself. They were certainly not after *her*. She had been in no danger, and they probably would not even have given her a second look, much less have paused to molest her, had she remained on the street and they had seen her as they dashed by. Well, they were gone now, in any case! She took a step forward toward the street—and stopped, a very tense and rigid little figure, as though rooted to the ground.

"For the pity of God, help me! But don't make a sound!"

The voice seemed to come from quite close at hand, almost it seemed from her very elbow. The words were French, but the accent was unmistakably English. Anne whirled around with a low, suppressed cry, and peered into the darkness of the lane. Close as she knew the voice to be, she could see nothing.

"Where are you?" she whispered quickly in English. "What is the matter?"

"You are English!" exclaimed the voice faintly. "An Englishwoman! Thank God! Here—I am here! On the ground close to the side of the house! I—I have been hurt. Shot, in fact. And—and rather badly, I'm afraid."

26

"Shot!" Anne repeated the word in a shocked, breathless way, as she hurriedly began to feel her way forward along the side of the house. She wasn't afraid any more of the darkness and the imaginings that the darkness held, or of those things that were not imaginings, but which brought terror because she did not understand what they were or what they meant. Here was the tangible, the concrete—a man had been shot here, hurt—and, most of all, here was some one who needed her help.

Just in front of her now, she could make out a shape huddled against the wall of the house; and in another instant she was on her knees beside the man. He was stretched out at full length on the ground, but now he raised himself on one elbow, though he kept the other hand tightly pressed to his side. Anne bent down a little closer, and, as the other lurched suddenly, she threw her arm around him to support him.

"This is awfully good of you. Some women would have shrieked and run, you know. I had to take a chance." There was something cool and debonair in the man's voice, weak though it was.

"You are bleeding," said Anne in a practical way. "Let me see if, first of all, I —"

"No earthly good!" said the man. "I've got a roll of shirt plugged up against the wound, and that's as effective as anything you could do for the moment."

"Yes, I suppose it is," agreed Anne quietly. "Well, then, we must get help at once. Either you must be taken to a doctor, or a doctor brought to you. There is no cab or any sort of conveyance to be had, so the only thing to do is to get some one in this house here to help us." She rose quickly to her feet. "I won't be a minute."

"Wait!" said the man sharply. "That is the last thing to do if you want to help me."

"Why, what do you mean?" demanded Anne.

"Just exactly what I say," the other answered.

"Whether they've finished me or not with this shot, I don't know, though I rather fancy they have—but if I'm found I'll get another bullet to put the question out of any doubt. To go into that house, or any other, would only result in putting them on my track again."

Anne, perplexed and anxious, stared at the other. "Was it those men who just ran by on the street who did this?" she asked.

"Yes; but they won't go far," the man replied. "I had the luck to double on them. I know this *quartier* well. They'll comb it before they're through—and how long do you think it would take before some one sneaked out of any rat-hole I went into here and spread the word around? They're all of the same breed!"

"Then what are we to do?" Anne's voice was steady, reliant now. "You can't stay here, because, as you say yourself, they'll find you sooner or later; and, above all, you must have help."

"I'm not quite at the end of my tether yet," said the man; "and I think, if you'd give me an arm, I could manage to get to a place I know of where, temporarily at least, I would be safe. But there is something quite a lot more important to be done first. I want to post a letter."

"A letter!" said Anne briskly. "That's rather simple, isn't it? You can give it to me, and I'll post it for you as soon as we get to this place you want to go where you can get attention."

"Not so simple," said the man. "I have neither envelope nor stamp."

"Well, we can get those, too," said Anne cheerfully. "Will you try to stand up now, and we'll see how we can get along?"

The man made no effort to move.

"The letter comes first," he said.

Anne stared again in a bewildered way.

"I don't understand," she said.

"There is nothing to understand," he replied, "except that I must post a letter before I do anything else, no matter what the consequences are." The man caught his breath suddenly, and pressed his hand heavily against his side. His voice was fainter, with a ring of pain in it, when he spoke again. "There is a little shop just around the corner two blocks away to the right, where you can get the envelope and the stamp—for God's sake, go and get them for me."

"But," protested Anne, "you are —"

"Please don't argue the matter," he interrupted hoarsely. "I'm not getting any stronger, and every minute is counting. You'll go, won't you? This is the only thing that counts. And, on the way, see if you can spot a post-box—that'll save time, too."

"Very well," said Anne a little hesitantly. "If you insist, and if it's as important as all that, I will. Give me your letter, then, and the address to which it is to be sent, and I will mail it for you before I come back."

"I'm sorry," said the man tersely, "very sorry— but that is impossible. I must post it myself. The address is as important as the letter."

"You mean," said Anne swiftly, "that you do not trust me?"

"If it must be put as bluntly as that—yes," he answered. "I trust no one."

"Really!" exclaimed Anne in sudden irritation, and with a stamp of her foot. "If I did not think you were very seriously wounded, I would leave you here to get out of your trouble the best way you could."

"And I would be the last one to blame you," returned the man calmly. "But you won't; for the end of my trouble would inevitably be the end of me. But first, however, I would have destroyed my letter— which perhaps would be the greater pity of the two."

The flash of anger and irritation that Anne had experienced died away. The man was suffering horribly, she knew, in spite of his cool and sangfroid manner. She was filled with pity for him, and she admired the grit and nerve he displayed. Who was he? What was this letter which was of such great importance that he preferred to risk his life rather than confide to her even the address to which it was to be sent? And why was he here like this? Who were those men who, a little while ago, had run so wildly and so blindly along the street out there in pursuit, according to his own statement, of this man beside her? She spoke almost subconsciously, as question after question flashed through her mind.

"Wait, then! I will come back as quickly as I can," she said; and, turning, hurried from the lane.

Anne gained the street and ran rapidly along. In the dim yellow glow of a street lamp, she made out a post-box at the first corner. That was part of her errand. She was conscious of a sense of relief that the box was so close to the lane. But suppose the man, even with her help, was unable to get that far? And even if he did, what about afterwards? She did not know. She had come to see Madame Frigon—and she was alone, in perhaps the worst *quartier* of Paris, with a man perhaps dying, certainly badly wounded, who was being hunted like a rat, and who was dependent upon her alone for his safety. If she could get help anywhere! A gendarme, for instance. But would she dare ask a gendarme, even if she could find one? She did not know what had led to the man being wounded, or what was behind it all. She might only be handing the man over to the police to answer for something that would leave him in very little better case (if not a worse one!) than if he were caught by those who had already wounded him and driven him into hiding.

She shook her head as she ran. She could do nothing but what she was doing. There was no alternative. And, anyway, he was an Englishman!

She met no one.

Around the second corner she found the shop to which the wounded man had directed her, a dingy, musty little place, run by an old man, who, as he served her, grumbled at the vileness of the night that kept everybody within doors and robbed him of his trade; and then Anne, with her small purchases, returned to the lane—again without meeting any one on the street.

She had been gone perhaps five minutes.

The man was stretched out on the ground exactly as she had left him. He greeted her eagerly.

"Did you get them?" he whispered excitedly.

"Yes," said Anne.

"Anybody see you?"

"No," Anne answered. "There wasn't a soul on the street."

"Good!" he ejaculated. "We'll beat them yet! Awfully good of you! I don't know how to thank you. Now, if you'll help me to prop myself up against the wall—"

Anne bent down, and, without a word, assisted the man to a sitting position.

"Now," he said, "the envelope and the stamp —and would you mind holding this improvised compress of mine in place for a moment so that I can use both hands?"

Anne again complied.

From his pocket the man took out what appeared in the darkness to be a folded sheet of paper and a pencil. He placed the paper in the envelope, sealed the latter, and laying it on his knee began to write.

Anne watched him with a growing feeling of uneasiness. There was something uncanny, weird, and unnatural in the situation—a man, badly wounded, writing in pitch blackness and certainly unable to see a word.

He seemed to read her thoughts.

"It *is* a bit dark," he said, with a short laugh; "but, it will be legible enough. Did you locate a post-box?"

Anne answered mechanically.

"Yes," she said, "I passed one on the way to the shop."

"All right!" Again the man laughed shortly. "Then that's our first port of call. If you'll help me to my feet, I'll try not to put too much weight on you as we go along."

"But there is absolutely no necessity for you to go to the box at all, unless it is on your way," said Anne with a sudden acerbity in her voice. "I will post your letter for you."

"Can't be done!" replied the man. "Positively it can't, you know. There is a street light out there— and, really, the writing's legible."

Anne's lips tightened.

"This is both unfair and absurd after what I have done for you!" she declared coldly. "I won't look at your letter. I haven't the slightest interest in it."

"Look here," said the man, "what's the use of talking about it? I'm in a bit of a beastly hole, and you can leave me in it if you like— but the letter doesn't go out of my hands unless I have to tear it up" . .
.

"Oh, very well, then," said Anne stiffly. "Since there is nothing else to be done, let us go."

With Anne's assistance the man got to his feet, and together, with his arm around her shoulder for support, they began to make their way unsteadily to the street.

"If any one sees us—I mean a casual passer-by," he jerked out with grim humour, "I'll be taken for a marital stew under convoy."

Anne ignored the remark. The man's weight upon her seemed to be growing heavier.

"I suppose it is quite useless to ask you even your name?" she suggested.

"My name?" he answered. "Not at all! A name doesn't matter. You can call me Kendall, if you like."

"And those men who were, or are, after you—do you mind telling me who they are?"

"Not at all," said the man readily. "They're a lot of Russians. As a matter of fact, they're a gang of Soviet agents." He stumbled suddenly, and almost fell. "Getting a bit done in," he said weakly. "Beastly shame! Where—where's the letter box?"

They had come abreast of it.

"Here," said Anne.

The man reached up and deposited his letter in the box—and for the first time Anne caught a meagre glimpse of his face. It was drawn and haggard and ghastly white; the face of a man of perhaps thirty-five or forty, she judged, though pain and pallour made it look like that of an old man. He was clean shaven, and, save that his garments were badly soiled, was well dressed. A wave of pity swept again over Anne—and creeping into her face came fear and consternation. The man could scarcely keep his feet.

He smiled at her reassuringly—and touched his lips, that were dry and fever-burned, with the tip of his tongue.

"I'll make it," he said, as though he had once more read her thoughts. "Don't you worry! It is not far. Carry on! We're going now to Mère Gigot's."

CHAPTER V   AT MÈRE GIGOT'S

THE darkness was abysmal. Anne was almost at the end of her strength. For the last little while she had had to support nearly the entire weight of her companion to keep him from falling. He still preserved his senses, for occasionally, in broken, gasping words, he blurted out directions; but it was obvious that he could go but little farther.

She did not know where they were, for, though the distance had not been great, they had turned and twisted through a veritable labyrinth of lanes and areaways and narrow, smelly passages that had brought utter confusion to her, and, besides, her attention had been wholly concentrated on her efforts to help the man. The whole situation was impossible. Again she had suggested, even pleaded with him, that she be allowed to apply for aid from the occupants of some house. It had seemed the only sane and logical thing to do, even if (though this was by no means certain) it led to his discovery by those who were searching for him, for the man was killing himself anyway by going on. He was literally dying on his feet, and the wonder of it was that he had not collapsed long ago. But he had refused with bitter emphasis to entertain her suggestion for an instant.

"'Go on! Go on!" he had gasped out. "I—I can make it. Safe there, I tell you! Mère Gigot's! Go on to Mère Gigot's!"

And so they had gone on.

Anne bit her lips to keep back a little cry of despair. She was utterly exhausted—the man's weight hurt her physically. How much farther was it? She couldn't go another yard. He couldn't, either. Yes, she could! Yes, he could! They must —because he refused to do anything else, and they must get somewhere. Suppose he became unconscious now! What would she do then? She couldn't actually carry the man, and she couldn't leave him a senseless heap in a back alleyway. What was the good of trying to think? But she could not help thinking, though her brain was beginning to flit irresponsibly from one thing to another. What would her father say if he knew? Thank Heaven, he was away in the country for a few days! What would certain ones, the rather fastidious and ultra-proper ones, amongst her circle of intimates say if they saw her in this black, ugly place from which there seemed to be no egress— saw her here stumbling helplessly along with a man who moaned and muttered

33

now, dragging at her neck. In the thick of the vilest dens of Paris where the apaches had their haunts—that's where she was!—and where, too, still an uglier class, the sewer-rats, were wont to come scuttling out from their foul abodes, not for a breath of cleaner air, but to prey upon any one who might be unfortunate enough to fall into their clutches!

If it were not much farther, perhaps they could crawl the rest of the way. . . . They couldn't go on. . . .

She had come to see Madame Frigon. It was very strange! There was something very horrible and very terrible about it too.

Her hair had fallen about her shoulders. She had long since lost her hat. The man had brushed it off. She had not been able to pick it up. The man would have fallen. And so she had left it. What did it matter—a hat? Some one would appropriate it without ado, and some woman would bedeck herself to the envy of her neighbours—or perhaps sell it for a few francs. It was an ill wind that blew nobody good!

Anne tried to straighten her drooping shoulders. The ache was unendurable; she felt as though her back were breaking under the load. Time and again they had stopped to rest, but the relief had been only transitory. Suddenly she turned a white, set face toward her companion. They had stopped again now. Usually he leaned against a wall to relieve her of his weight; but now he was slipping to the ground as though his legs had gone limp beneath him.

With a low, quick cry, Anne snatched desperately at the man's arms and shoulders, but she could not hold him. It was the end. It was what she had known would happen. He lay motionless at her feet.

She leaned over and called to him anxiously. At first he made no answer, and then she heard him speak, but his voice was faint and weak, and, besides, the words ran together, and she could not make out what he said.

"Don't try to speak," she said, and with an effort kept her voice steady and under control. "Try to understand me. We can't go any farther. You must let me get help now from somewhere no matter what happens."

"No—farther," mumbled the man. His voice grew a little stronger. "That's right! I—I told you, I'd make it. We're here."

"Here?" repeated Anne. "What do you mean by 'here?' "

"Mère Gigot's! La Dame Gigot's!" he said. "It is here."

Anne stared about her. In the utter darkness she could see nothing. That there were walls of houses interspersed with the fences of refuse-strewn and diminutive backyards abutting on both sides of the narrow alleyway, she knew instinctively, but there was not the faintest glimmer of light from anywhere. But, then, the man's mind was wandering now, of course.

"Try to understand me," she repeated quietly and distinctly. "I am going to get help from the first house or the first person I find, and—"

"But I tell you we're here!" The man's voice was querulous, impatient now. "This is Mère Gigot's. Can't you see?"

Anne stared around her again.

"No; I can't," she said blankly. "Where?"

"Behind me," said the man. "The shed! Can't you see the shed? All you have to do is to open the door."

Anne stepped past the prostrate figure, and, groping out with her hands, touched what seemed like the rough boarding of a fence. She felt over it in all directions without meeting any indication of a door.

The man was struggling up on his elbow again.

"Push on it!" he said.

Anne obeyed. The boarding gave under her hands quite easily— and so silently that it startled her.

The man was crawling forward now.

"Go in, and hold the door open," he directed. "I can make it, all right."

Again Anne obeyed. She sensed rather than saw the man crawl past her.

He spoke again from her feet.

"Now shut the door, and help me up again."

Anne closed the door. It had been dark out in the alleyway; in here it was as though one were blind. She could not see even the outline of the man that she knew to be within a few feet of her. If this was Mère Gigot's it was a very strange place indeed for a domicile, or, indeed, even for an approach to one!

If it had not been for the man's obviously intimate acquaintance with the location of a door where there was little indication of one, and the significant silence with which that door had opened and closed, she would have thought that he had merely stumbled blindly upon a doorway, his mind obsessed with the idea that he had reached his destination. The intense blackness seemed to stifle and choke her

—seemed almost to close around her throat and *clutch* at it. And suddenly she liked the situation and her surroundings less than at any time before that night! Who was Mère Gigot? *What* was this place he called La Dame Gigot's?

"Help me up!" repeated the man from the floor.

Anne fought a sharp and decisive battle with herself. She was afraid now; afraid of this place, and particularly of what it promised; afraid of this Mère Gigot—but she was more afraid of being a traitor to the moral obligation she owed this man to see him finally in some one's hands, where, if it were not already too late, he would receive medical aid and attention.

"If this is Mère Gigot's," she said steadily, "tell me where to find her, and I'll bring her here to you. You mustn't walk another step."

"You! Go into Mère Gigot's alone!" he exclaimed. "No fear! I wouldn't let you—it wouldn't be playing the game. Besides, you'd never find the way. Help me up, I tell you! It's only a yard or so—and—I'm fit as they make 'em now. We've won—beaten 'em! I feel like a new man!" He caught at her knees and began to drag himself up. Anne had no choice but to help him to his feet. And it was true—he *did* seem stronger. His voice had almost a buoyant ring. It was merely nervous excitement and exhilaration, of course, but it was a renewed strength, no matter what its origin, that would not be denied.

They stumbled forward. There seemed to be a litter of all manner of things on the floor, as though the place had long been in utter disuse. It had been difficult enough to walk out there in the lanes and alleyways, trying to support her companion's sagging, lurching form, but now Anne found herself tripping over some obstruction at almost every step. The man laughed out shrilly, unnaturally.

"Mère Gigot's portico!" he laughed. "D'ye hear that? Mère Gigot's portico! A bit of all-right! The *agents de police* would pay a franc or two to know about it."

Anne shivered a little. The police! Why should the police be interested?

"There's a way in from here—underground, you know." The man's voice was high-pitched, jerky, as unnatural as his laugh. "But I'm afraid I couldn't stick the ladder, and I fancy the yard's safe enough since we haven't been followed."

Anne made no answer. She felt the fresh air in her face. The man had opened a door. They were out in the open again. It was too dark to distinguish anything except that they seemed to be amongst a nest of buildings, and that now, from here and there, a window light gleamed faintly.

The man was strangely wrought up, eager now, forcing the pace, like one inspired by the sight of his goal, and yet fearful that even at the last he might not reach it except by a final and desperate spurt.

They crossed, lurching, staggering, swaying, a short open space, and then Anne saw a street light. It was abortive in the mist and almost useless as a source of illumination, but it served at least one purpose—Anne realized that the shed through which they had just come must have made the corner of the alleyway and the street. The next moment they were on the street itself; then her companion pushed a door open, and they stumbled forward across the threshold. The door, seemingly of its own volition, closed behind them.

An instant Anne stood there confused, trying to visualize her surroundings in the sudden transition from darkness to light. It was all a blur at first. There was some sort of a bizarre scene way down *below* her; and there was a hubbub of noise, and the sound of many voices— some raised in ribald song and laughter. Her vision cleared. She was standing on a sort of landing, or platform, upon which the street door opened, and, from this landing, leading down along the side of the wall, was a short flight of some dozen stone, or cement stairs. There had once been a balustrade, she noticed, but this had been almost entirely broken away. The place was neither more nor less than a cellar, the walls had once been whitewashed, but now were a grimy yellow, and were scrawled all over with crude and questionable drawings, while here and there *risque* posters in blatant colours flaunted themselves. The light was supplied by six or seven ill-trimmed lamps pendant from the ceiling. The air was vile, almost nauseating, from the smoking lamps and the odour of spilled liquor and stale tobacco. Strewn about the floor without any attempt at order were a number of small tables—some of them unoccupied; but at least a score of men were in the den, drinking, playing cards, or shouting and singing at the top of their lungs and banging in tempo on the table-tops with bottles. Anne drew in her breath quickly. She did not like their looks—one glance was enough to classify them as apaches of the most abandoned type.

It had seemed a long time, but she realized that it could have been no more than a matter of seconds since she had stepped in from the street, as now, over the din from below her, stilling it instantly, and causing every eye to focus upward to where she stood at the head of the stairs, the wounded man, who but an instant ago had been clinging desperately to her again with his arm flung around her shoulders, suddenly drew himself erect, and waved his hand—and laughed wildly.

"Salut, mes amis!" he shouted. *"Vive la Dame Gigot!* I am here with only one little hole in me —a Mère trifle that—" He reeled and pitched forward.

With a terrified cry, Anne snatched at him— missed him—and then, involuntarily, her hands covered her eyes to shut out the sight, as, like a sack of meal, a limp thing, the man went tumbling down the stairs, rolling over and over, bumping with ever increasing rapidity from one tread to another.

A roar of voices welled up to her from below— cries, oaths, excited exclamations. She found herself running down the stairs. A dozen men were jostling, pushing, swaying around the bottom step. Faces, some threatening, some with a smile that boldly appraised her for herself quite irrespective of anything else, formed a ring around her. Some one grasped her roughly by the arm; voices bawled in her ears demanding who she was, how she came there—a babel of questions all of the same tenor.

A drunken voice hiccoughed out over the others:

"Imagine! *Une petite aristocrate!* Imagine an aristocrat at La Dame Gigot's! *Oh, la la!"*

"Hold your tongue, *vieux polisson!"* snapped a woman's voice.

Anne, her face set, her eyes straight in front of her, paid no attention. The circle opened for her. On the floor, the wounded man lay motionless with closed eyes.

Two of the den's clientele were bending over the Englishman.

"He's dead!" said one of these, with a callous shrug of his shoulders; and added facetiously: "A pretty little affair—eh? A murder. Shall we say good-night to the adorable Mère Gigot, or shall we stay to drink a bottle with the dirty little pigs of police who will be here the moment they hear of this?"

"You are wrong," said the other, with a short laugh; "he's breathing, so he can't be dead yet. That is the trouble with the little lead pill—one does not always die at once, and sometimes not at all. For me—bah!—the knife every time! It is always sure if you know where to strike!"

"Baboons! Clowns! Shut your mouths, imbeciles!" It was the harsh female voice again. "If he is not dead, go and get some water; and you, *balbuzard*"—this to the last speaker—"bring me some cognac, and if you take any from the bottle for yourself, *nom d'un forçat,* I will slit your tongue for you!"

Anne felt herself brushed incontinently aside. A woman of huge stature, with arms akimbo, stood staring down at the figure on the floor. It was Mère Gigot, of course. Anne could not see the woman's face, but even Mère Gigot's back was not prepossessing. The woman should have been a man, for she obviously had the strength of one. Her neck was thick and corded with muscles; her arms—the sleeves of the loose and dirty *peignoir* that she wore were rolled up almost to the armpits—were coarse, unlovely, muscle-knotted like her neck.

"Name of a name!" muttered Mère Gigot, and drew in a long breath with a sharp, hissing sound. "Name of all the devils from the pit! It is the English dandy! It is the Englishman, Kendall!" She whirled suddenly around and stared at Anne.

Anne instinctively drew back. Mère Gigot's face was even less reassuring than her figure— there was something even repulsive about it. It was *hard*—with no single feature to soften it.

The eyes were so pale that they were almost white; the lips were thin and quite bloodless—there was something cruel about the lips. But then there was something cruel about the whole face. The woman was middle-aged—slovenly. Her hair was tawny in colour, somewhat matted, and obviously unwashed.

"Bézain was right," she said sharply. "You are a little aristocrat. But the Englishman there is not an aristocrat. He is not of your kind. What is he to you, that you come here together like this?"

Anne shook her head.

"He is nothing to me," she explained quietly, "except that he is a man whom I found wounded, and who asked for help."

"Ah!" exclaimed Mère Gigot. "So you are English, too—though you speak French well. So, you only found him, eh?—you two English people! Well, you will tell me about that in a minute, and where you *found* him, and how he came to be shot, for I have an idea that my pretty young lady knows a great deal more than she pretends. But first there is another little question that you will answer. Do the police pigs know anything about this—eh? Have you been followed here?"

"I feel sure, from what he said, that the police know nothing about it," Anne answered. "And I am quite positive that we were neither seen nor followed here by any one."

Anne felt the other's eyes boring into her; and, curiously, what blue there was in them seemed to fade away, leaving them horribly colourless. And suddenly she winced under the pressure of the woman's vise-like grip, as Mère Gigot without warning grasped her roughly by the shoulder.

"Tell the truth!" snarled Mère Gigot threateningly.

Anne drew herself up.

"I'm telling the truth," she said coldly.

For a moment the colourless eyes held upon Anne's face, and then Mère Gigot, with a shrug of her shoulders, laughed unpleasantly.

"Yes, I believe you," she said coarsely; "and it is a good thing, perhaps, for you that I do. I cannot afford to have the police stick their noses into any *bagarre* like this at Mère Gigot's. You understand? They go too far once they begin, and there are little matters here that—eh?—well, what you don't know won't hurt you any more than it will them! It is bad enough as it is. Since a month now, one or another of them has come mincing in every few days, all smiles and slobbers—*les sales coquins!*—to pay me compliments that would not deceive any one, and to drink a bottle of wine. Bah! As if they wanted to drink Mère Gigot's wine—though I charge them nothing for it! And now to-night—"

Mère Gigot broke off suddenly, and half turned away.

Anne instinctively glanced at the wounded man on the floor. He still showed no signs of returning consciousness, though several of the apaches were obviously doing what they could for him—they had a basin of water and some cloths now, and the man Mère Gigot had sent for the cognac was trying to force some of the brandy between the Englishman's lips. Why didn't they send for a doctor? —and at once!

Anne turned sharply toward Mère Gigot—and the protest on her lips died unuttered. She had supposed that Mère Gigot, too, had been watching the scene on the floor, perhaps with a wary eye on the disposal of the cognac, but Mère Gigot was looking in quite another direction—and Mère Gigot's face was red and convulsed with fury, and her mouth worked as though she was striving to say something while her fury rendered her speechless.

40

Anne's eyes followed the direction of Mère Gigot's.

A man, a miserable little figure, with a thin, pasty face, and a black velvet student's cap hanging over one ear, and to whom no one else in the place seemed to be paying any attention, was sidling stealthily up the flight of stairs toward the street door.

And then La Dame Gigot found her voice.

"Stop him!" she shrieked. *"Le sacré mouchard!* It is Franchon— eh? Ah, you dirty spy! So, we know you now for what you are, eh? You would go for the police, would you? Stop him! He is a spy, I tell you! Stop him!"

A howl of execration answered Mère Gigot's words; there was a rush for the stairs—and the figure, already halfway up, gave a startled cry, and leaped suddenly for the top.

And then the door from the street opened and closed, and another figure stood on the landing, blocking the escape of the man that Mère Gigot had denounced as a spy.

Anne felt the blood suddenly leave her cheeks. There was something so unnatural happening now that for a moment it terrified her. The execrations had instantly died away; there was utter silence. The rush for the stairs had halted as though by magic; no one moved. The man that Mère Gigot had called Franchon was crouched in a frightened way against the wall, his hands clawing out on each side of him. Anne's eyes were irresistibly drawn to the figure on the landing above Franchon a man, quite tall, enveloped in a long black cloak under which both hands were hidden, who stood there motionless. He wore a round black hat with a wide brim. Under the brim of this hat his face seemed to be all beard, a black, heavy beard— except for the eyes that, even at that distance, glowed like living fire as they reflected the light.

It was the man Franchon who spoke. It was only a babbled word and uttered scarcely above his breath, but in the eerie stillness it reached Anne distinctly.

"Fire-Eyes!" the spy babbled.

CHAPTER VI   FIRE-EYES

FIRE-EYES! Anne was staring up at the figure on the top of the landing in a half-startled, half-fascinated way now. Yes, he was in appearance exactly as Madame Frigon had described him—only—only he seemed even more sinister, somehow, than she had pictured him from the old woman's description.

Fire-Eyes broke the silence.

"What is the trouble, *mes amis?*" he inquired softly.

"Trouble!" The word came in a hoarse scream from Mère Gigot. She forced a passage for herself to the foot of the stairs, flinging those in her way to right and left. *"That* is the trouble!" She pointed to the man cringing against the wall a few steps below Fire-Eyes. "A man comes in here shot, wounded—perhaps it will be murder— I do not know—for he is still alive. Look!" She turned and pointed excitedly to where the Englishman lay on the floor. "And that vile *mouchard*"— she was shaking both fists furiously now at Franchon— "tries to sneak away to inform the police. He is a spy! That is the trouble, and it is enough—to bring the police here!"

Fire-Eyes stared down the stairs at the figure of the Englishman, stared for a long minute while the silence held again, and then for the first time he moved—he took a step very slowly and deliberately toward Franchon.

With a scream Franchon backed away.

"So you are a spy, a police leech, are you?" purred Fire-Eyes. "That is very bad, *mon Franchon!* Well, you know what we do with spies."

Fire-Eyes descended another step; Franchon retreated as before. Down the stairs the two men went; Fire-Eyes without haste, but closing the gap between them for Franchon was moving more and more slowly as though, literally, a paralysis of his limbs were creeping upon him—and Franchon was a pitiable looking object, moving sideways, his back pressed hard against the wall; his pasty-white face turned toward Fire-Eyes; his lips working, but making no sound.

No one else in the miserable dive stirred now. To Anne it seemed that she could not have moved an inch from where she stood—that it was as though the power to perform any physical act had been suddenly taken away from her. She was conscious of a horrible sense of fascination, as she watched the two figures on the stairs—the slow, deliberate movement of Fire-Eyes drawing closer and ever closer to the other; the cringing, trembling figure of Franchon, whose movements were becoming more and more impotent with every step. Once, in the "zoo," she had seen a rabbit and a snake—she could not think of anything else. She remembered the snake's eyes, the rhythmic-swaying head; she remembered the fear-stricken, shaking little animal—and she had run from the place with a cry of utter abhorrence, her whole soul in revolt-—she had not waited for the end. She wanted to run now—but she could not move.

Franchon stood still now—quite motionless, except that he trembled more violently than before. He seemed to be pinioned to the wall, fixed, immovable, merely by the magnetism of the other's eyes.

Anne's heart seemed suddenly to stop its beat. Fire-Eyes, too, had halted—just within arm's reach of the other—and from under the cloak came glittering a knife in Fire-Eyes' hand—a long, sharp-pointed, cruel thing. Anne wanted to scream. Something welled up in her throat and choked her. She could make no sound.

Fire-Eyes' movements were still without haste —there was something hideous, abominable in his very *deliberation.* What were the words Madame Frigon had used, when she had told about the girl Tisotte?—Oh God!—"like one who was doing no more than if he were lighting a cigarette."

And Franchon made no offer of resistance. His hands out-spread on either side of him, remained flattened against the wall, as though held there by a hypnotic spell.

And then across each of Franchon's cheeks, Fire-Eyes' knife, cutting deep and long, made two criss-cross slashes—and the red came streaming from the pasty face where the flesh hung loose.

"Now go!" said Fire-Eyes in the same soft, purring tones that he had used before. "And if tonight an *agent de police* shows his face around here, then to-morrow the knife will cut lower than the cheeks!"

The spell was suddenly broken. Screaming, clutching at his face with both hands, Franchon stumbled up the stairs, and, lunging blindly through the door to the street, disappeared.

Howls of applause came from the assembled apaches.

"*. . . À bas les mouchards! . . . Vive Fire-Eyes! . . .*"

Anne groped her way to the side of the wall for support.

She was sick, weak, faint. The man was a fiend. He wasn't human. He was a fiend.

But she could not take her eyes from him.

He came down the remaining steps, walked over to where the Englishman lay, looked down for a moment at the other's face—and then suddenly he laughed in a low, cool way, and swung around to Mère Gigot.

"So *this* is the man, is it, who has been shot?" he said smoothly. "Well, then, it is a great stroke of luck, *ma belle Gigot*—a great stroke of luck that he came here! He should have a little paper in his possession, *le petit gaillard!*" He stooped down, and, deftly and swiftly, went through the unconscious man's pockets. Then, empty-handed, he swung around again and fixed his piercing eyes on Mère Gigot. "But there is no paper here! Perhaps *you* can explain that?"

Mère Gigot, her huge hands on her hips, shook her head.

"I can explain nothing!" Mère Gigot's snarl and truculency were gone; her voice was meek, almost fawning. "He came only a minute ahead of monsieur. That is the truth. I swear it. Nothing has been taken from him. I do not know of any paper. I can explain nothing. Ask *her!*"

Anne felt herself now the target of the man's eyes. She drew herself up, and forced herself to meet his gaze—but they made her shiver, those eyes. They were like black, turbulent pools of evil, pools of some fiery nature that seemed to emit shafts of light which darted out, swift as the thrust of a serpent's fang, to stab and burn her.

And yet, somehow, for a single instant his eyes seemed to falter as they met her direct gaze, and for an instant too—if it were not pure overwrought imagination on her part—there was a quick, startled, muscular contraction of the man's lips. But it was gone—if, indeed, it had ever existed— as swiftly as it had come.

"A lady!" murmured Fire-Eyes with a profound and mocking bow. He turned to Mère Gigot. "Your fame, *ma belle,* has obviously gone abroad, since already those of fashion seek you out. It is time you moved to the boulevards and lined your walls with mirrors, and upholstered your chairs with plush—preferably in red!"

Mère Gigot made no direct answer; but the grins on the faces of the ragged and decidedly unwholesome crowd, that had now pressed closely and inquisitively around in a circle—the only clientele that Mère Gigot would ever boast—evidently enraged her. She swept out her arms, as though they were a pair of flails, and began to beat about her.

"Canaille!" she screamed, as she scattered and drove the men back to their tables. "Keep your donkeys' ears for your own affairs! Name of a thousand little pigs! Leave the business of Mère Gigot alone!"

"And you, *mes amis,*" directed Fire-Eyes calmly to the two men who were still attempting to revive the Englishman, "carry that fellow into the back room and leave him there. As for the rest of you, you will drink a little bottle with Fire-Eyes—eh? *Ça va?*"

A thunder of applause greeted the invitation. Mère Gigot rubbed her palms together—over a gold piece of twenty francs that Fire-Eyes had thrust into her hands.

Anne stepped forward—the Englishman was being carried toward the rear of the cellar.

"That man should have a doctor at once—without another instant's delay," she said resolutely.

Fire-Eyes measured her with a long glance.

"But, yes! Naturally!" he said tersely. He spoke for a moment in an undertone to Mère Gigot, then turned again to Anne. "That will be attended to," he said brusquely. "Meanwhile"— he pointed to the rear door through which the wounded man had just been carried—"you will go in there, too, mademoiselle, if you please. There is a certain little matter to be settled, and a few questions to be asked."

Anne looked around the den. The place seemed suddenly even more repulsive than it had been before. The two men who had carried the Englishman away were returning from the back room. She did not like the idea of that back room. She wanted to get away now—to get away from the horribleness of the whole place. She had done what she could for the wounded man, and they had promised to get a doctor for him at once. She could do no more.

"I would prefer to answer any questions here," she said quietly. "And please make them as few and as brief as possible. I am anxious to get home now, as quickly as I can."

"And I would prefer that you should answer them—in there!" said Fire-Eyes coldly.

"Go!" snarled Mère Gigot imperatively, and, catching Anne roughly by the shoulder, propelled her violently toward the rear room. "Do you give orders here because you are a lady? *Nom de Dieu!* Who cares whether you want to get home or not?"

The door of the rear room closed behind the three of them—and Mère Gigot leaned with her back against it, a sneer on her lips, her arms akimbo again.

Anne stood with clenched hands in the centre of the floor. It was, perhaps, Mère Gigot's bedroom—anyway there was a bed here, a very dirty bed, and the Englishman lay upon it. Anne shuddered a little. It was a filthy place—even more filthy, if that were possible, than the drinking hell outside. Suddenly she looked with a sort of startled curiosity around her, as she recalled the Englishman's statement that there was a secret entrance into Mère Gigot's dive. Was it here? There did not seem to be any other room beyond this one, for there was no sign of any door except the one by which she had entered.

Fire-Eyes fixed her with his eyes. They seemed to come nearer— like glowing orbs constantly increasing in size—nearer and nearer— and yet she was quite sure that the man himself did not move. She forced her will to combat the mesmeric effect they were producing upon her.

"What is your name? Where do you live?" demanded Fire-Eyes curtly.

"My name is Anne Walton," Anne answered. She gave her address.

"That's quite a long way from here—in more ways than one," said Fire-Eyes gratingly. "Is it a habit of yours to frequent neighbourhoods such as this at night with, say"—he jerked his head toward the figure on the bed—"that man as your companion?"

"No; it is not!" replied Anne icily. "And so far as that man is concerned, I never saw him in my life until to-night."

"Perhaps mademoiselle will be good enough to tell us, then," inquired Fire-Eyes, his voice unpleasantly devoid of inflexion, "how she came to be with him here?"

For a moment Anne did not answer. She loathed, detested, and, in a sense, she feared this man who stood here prodding her with questions. She had no need to remember now the tales that Madame Frigon had told of him; she had seen with her own eyes the horrible and bestial thing he had done out there on the stairs—the inhuman callousness he had exhibited in committing the act. Her impulse was to turn her back upon him. To speak to him was revolting. But her common sense prevailed. She would gain nothing by refusing to answer, and she was very fully aware that she was helplessly in his power—and in the power of that sexless creature garbed as a woman who stood guard there at the door.

"I came to the *quartier"* she said, "to bring some provisions to—" She caught herself up sharply.

She had been about to say "Madame Frigon." But she remembered Madame Frigon's very evident terror concerning this man—a terror of perhaps being some day recognized again. It would be quite as fatal then for Madame Frigon, if this man chanced to recognize the name.

Fire-Eyes' nostrils had distended slightly. There was a sneer on his lips.

"We are at the point, I believe, where you are on your way somewhere with some provisions," he prompted caustically.

"Yes," said Anne hastily. "I had a basket of things for an old woman, who is one of a number of poor people that I often visit, and for whom I try to do what I can. I dismissed the cabman who drove me down here because I am quite sure he intended to rob me. When I left to go home, there was no other cab to be had, and so I had to walk. After I had gone a few blocks, I heard shots; and a little farther on, I heard men racing along the sidewalk toward me. To avoid them, I stepped into a lane; and then, when they had passed, and just as I was going out to the street again, that man on the bed there, who had also been hiding in the lane, called to me, and I went to him and found that he had been wounded."

"How amazingly *accidental!"* observed Fire-Eyes sarcastically. "I would not spoil your story by questioning it for an instant—and, after all, I am interested only in a certain paper that your *chance* acquaintance carried. And since, according to your own story, he was in hiding and had not been caught, and since Mère Gigot swears that nothing was taken from him here, and since it is nevertheless not in his possession now, the deduction is fairly obvious, is it not, mademoiselle? Give it to me at once!"

Anne drew back. The man was advancing toward her, those venomous eyes were narrowing— no, not narrowing—*widening* on her again.

"I have no paper," she said evenly. "But I do not deny that I know he had one—or, at least, what he called a letter. If that is what you want it will do you very little good, for he posted it himself."

"Ah!" drawled Fire-Eyes. "So he posted it, did he? And when did he post it?"

"Before he came here," Anne replied crisply.

"I went to a store and got an envelope and a stamp at his request, and brought them back to him in the lane. He addressed the envelope there, and afterwards posted it himself. He would not even let me put it in the box for fear that I would see the address."

Fire-Eyes snarled suddenly.

"You tell it well, but it is rather hard to believe, mademoiselle. But we will soon see, however, whether you are telling the truth or not." He turned and motioned to Mère Gigot. "Search her!" he ordered laconically. "And search her *well!*"

Anne drew still farther back and found herself against the wall. She could not retreat any farther. Mère Gigot was advancing, cackling shrilly, making horrible grimaces.

"You beast!" cried Anne passionately. "You"— the woman had caught her in a crushing grip, and was commencing, despite her struggles, to tear at her clothes—"you—you loathesome beast!"

"Wait!" Fire-Eyes' voice came harshly, abruptly. "Our friend on the bed seems to be coming to life. Perhaps *he* will tell us whether mademoiselle is lying or not."

Anne, breathing heavily, her small hands clenched, her face flushed with anger and humiliation, leaned back against the wall as Mère Gigot released her. She could hear the Englishman mumbling— incoherently it seemed—as though unconscious and delirious. Fire-Eyes was bending over the bed.

"What does he say?" shrilled Mère Gigot.

"The paper! . . . The paper!" The Englishman's voice rose high-pitched and quavering. "Bowled 'em out . . . Stumped 'em. . . . Posted it . . . Get it to-morrow . . . A bit of all-right, what? . . ."

"Get some more cognac!" snapped Fire-Eyes.

Mère Gigot hurriedly left the room.

"And as for you, mademoiselle"—Fire-Eyes swung suddenly around from the bed—"since it would appear from what he says—and *he* is in no condition to concoct lies—that your story is true, you may go. So, go home!" His voice grew silky. "You have been very fortunate. I trust you will continue to be so. I am sure you will, if you do not permit yourself to forget our little Franchon—who was not so fortunate. Franchon had a tongue that swung too loosely on its hinges. For mademoiselle's sake, I would like to believe she quite understands that to-night has never existed. And I would like to suggest that hereafter mademoiselle confine her visits and her attentions strictly to—the poor." His voice hardened suddenly. "You understand? One word of what you have either seen or heard to-night, and you will have cause to envy Franchon as long as you live; though, in that case, I fear you would not have very long to live. I bid you good-night, mademoiselle!"

In a dazed, uncertain way, Anne made her way to the street—and hours later, it seemed, and miles and miles away, it seemed, she found a fiacre that finally drove her home.

§

It was midnight. The Englishman on the bed in the back room of Mère Gigot's dive ceased his mumbling, his limbs jerked spasmodically once or twice—and he lay still.

Mère Gigot made a clucking sound with her tongue against the roof of her mouth. As an afterthought she crossed herself.

"Dead!" said Mère Gigot.

Fire-Eyes drew his cloak around his shoulders, and rose from the chair upon which he had been sitting.

"It has taken longer than I thought it would," he said indifferently.

"Monsieur would not let me send for a doctor," muttered Mère Gigot. "Perhaps if—"

"You are a fool!" said Fire-Eyes contemptuously. "It would only have been another mouth to close, and that is the hardest kind of a mouth to close— a doctor's mouth. It would not suit me at all that a certificate of death should be sent to the *Hotel de Ville.*"

"That is true!" Mère Gigot clucked with her tongue again. She looked cunningly, inquiringly at Fire-Eyes.

"Certainly—some time before daylight!" said Fire-Eyes curtly. "You can choose a couple of men out there who can be trusted to keep their mouths shut—and who will know what to expect if they let their tongues wag!"

"There are Balbuzard and Bezain," said Mère Gigot with a shrug of her shoulders. "It is not the first time they have done the job."

"Pay them, then—and yourself," said Fire-Eyes as he extended some gold—but now there was a threatening note in his voice. "But see that there is no bungling—see that all trace of him *disappears.* He has no friends and no family to make inquiries about him. That end of it is safe. See that *your* end is safe! If he happened to be found floating in the Seine, for instance, there is nothing more certain than that you and Balbuzard and Bezain would shortly after be found there also!"

Mère Gigot clutched avariciously at the gold. "Have no fear, monsieur!" She laughed harshly. "Mère Gigot does not do things that way. It will be—poof!—like that!—as though he had never been! But what of the girl, the *milady?* What if she comes here? What if she talks?"

"If she comes here, that will be your business," Fire-Eyes answered coldly. "If she talks elsewhere, it will be mine." He stepped to the door. "It is all understood, Mère Gigot?"

"But—yes!" Mère Gigot clucked with her tongue again, and jingled the gold pieces from one hand to the other. *"Nom d'un sacre nom d'un nom* —have no fear, monsieur!"

A thin and ugly smile curled Fire-Eyes' lips.

"I will leave you to your little affairs, then." He opened the door. *"Bon soir, ma belle Gigot!"* The door closed behind him.

§

Anne had passed an almost sleepless night. She rose in the morning unrefreshed, tired, her mind tormented. The events of the preceding evening clung to her like a constantly recurring nightmare. What had happened to the Englishman? Was he better; was he worse? Was it any further an affair of hers? Hadn't she been warned not to interfere any more—to forget that the evening had ever existed? But she couldn't forget. It was not an idle warning that she had received. She knew that. She had been told to remember Franchon! As long as she lived she would never forget that horrible sight. She saw it now—just as though it were taking place again before her eyes.

She pressed her hands against her aching temples. Her father was away. She was alone. She could not ask his advice. If the Englishman died, it was murder, and the police would start an investigation. How could she keep quiet under such circumstances, no matter what the consequences to herself might be? What right had she to keep quiet? *Those eyes!* She shivered. Yes, her duty was clear—and she would do it. But if, on the other hand, the Englishman recovered—well, that was different. She would be justified then in considering it the

Englishman's personal affair; and she could leave it alone with a clear conscience. But she must know. Her mind would never be at rest until she did.

Anne dressed and went out.

Mère Gigot's proved, after all, not very hard to find. A few inquiries brought Anne to the door, though it bore no sign, and, entering, she found herself standing again on the sort of platform at the head of the stairs, where she had stood the night before. It was bright sunshine outside, but there, was no daylight within, and the place looked even more drab and forbidding than when she had seen it last, for now only a single lamp was burning. There were no customers—Mère Gigot's clientele was not of the sort that went abroad in daylight— but Anne could see the woman herself busy at the *comptoir* below her.

"Madame Gigot!" Anne called.

Mère Gigot looked up.

"Ah—you!" she exclaimed, with an insolent stare. "So you are back, eh?" She crossed the floor to the foot of the stairs. "Well, what do you want?"

"I came to ask how that Englishman is who was here with me last night," said Anne quietly. "And, if it is possible, I would also like to see him."

"Ah—your Englishman!" Mère Gigot clucked her tongue, grinned, and shook her head. "Well, your Englishman is all right, but you cannot see him because he has gone away."

"Gone away?" repeated Anne. "Where?"

Mère Gigot shook her head.

"How should I know? I do not keep the address of every one who comes here. And I do not ask too many questions. The doctor came— and in a little while your Englishman was—poof!—like himself again. The doctor said the wound was nothing at all—what do you call it?—a—a flesh wound. It was only because the Johnny Bull had lost so much blood. After that your Englishman sent for two of his friends, and they took him away."

"Then—then you are sure," said Anne earnestly, "that he is quite all right? That he will recover?"

"But, of course!" Mère Gigot planted her hands on her hips—her attitude was one of impatience and exasperation at being called upon to answer the same question twice. *"Sacre nom,* have I not just told you so? Naturally, he will recover!"

"Oh, I am so glad!" said Anne fervently.

"Bah!" snorted Mère Gigot, with a philosophical shrug of her shoulders. "These little affairs happen every day. They are nothing—nothing at all!"

A weight seemed to have been lifted from Anne's shoulders. She went away light-hearted.

BOOK II:

The Chase

CHAPTER I   TWO MONTHS LATER

THE bungalow was perched high up on the hillside. Over the tree-tops, that in perspective looked like a vast green tapestry of intricate and wonderful design, and that changed kaleidoscopically as the sun played hide and seek with the drifting clouds, could be seen in the far distance, some six or seven miles away, the harbour of Suva and the open sea. Of the town itself, nestling along the ocean front, nothing was discernible, save where, here and there, a tiny patch of white indicated a dwelling on Flagstaff Hill.

On the verandah a man lay stretched out in a reclining chair. He was dapper and in immaculate white. At first glance he appeared to be a man well on in the sixties; but upon closer acquaintance one was apt to revise that opinion. There was a certain vivacity about Mr. Henry Walton, a litheness both physical and mental, that argued in favour of the fact that the snow-white hair had attained its colour prematurely rather than with the natural passing of the years. He was clean shaven, and wore rather elegantly and not unbecomingly a pair of gold pince-nez with amber lenses, which gave to his eyes a nondescript colour somewhere between black and brown.

On the arm of his chair stood a tumbler at which he stared with half-closed eyes, and which he kept twisting rapidly with his fingers—as though intent upon the degree of deftness with which he could propel the bobbing half of a lime around the rim of the glass. Presently he raised the tumbler to his lips, but set it down again abruptly and rose suddenly to his feet, as, from near at hand, there sounded the blast of a motor horn, and coincidentally, Anne, a fresh, brown-haired vision in white, appeared in the doorway of the bungalow.

Mr. Walton inspected the girl's figure critically— and a little quizzically.

"I imagine, Anne," he said, with a glance in the direction of the road, which was hidden by the trees, "I imagine that was Donald Lane I heard just now."

The girl smiled.

"I imagine it was, father," she answered demurely.

"And where away this afternoon?" Mr. Walton inquired. "I see you have your hat on."

Anne crossed the verandah and perched herself gracefully on the low railing.

"Oh, just a run up in the hills," she answered. "Nowhere in particular."

"H'm!" drawled Mr. Walton. "'Nowhere in particular!'—has it got to that stage in one short week?"

Anne looked at him quickly, the faintest tinge of colour dyeing her cheeks.

"What do you mean?" she asked.

"My dear"—Mr. Walton smiled broadly and shrugged his shoulders—"you know what I mean. The chronic symptom of growing intimacy! You are seeing a great deal of young Lane—er—a very great deal of John Crane's nephew."

"You are absurd, father," Anne said a little sharply. "He has been extremely nice to me, and I like him tremendously as a friend. I have never thought of him in any other way."

"No; of course not!" Henry Walton picked up the tumbler again, and sipped at it now with exaggerated deliberation. "One never does," he murmured. His eyes smiled over the rim of the glass. "It's strange, isn't it?—but it's as old as the ages. One never does—until a certain psychological moment arrives. And then—" He paused to sip at his glass again.

"And then?" Anne elevated her eyebrows.

"Blooey!" said Mr. Walton calmly. "That's American. I got it from Mr. Lane himself. It means—er—all manner of things. Expressive— very!"

"Very, I'm sure!" said Anne tersely. A puzzled look came into her eyes. "I—I can't understand why you should have brought the subject up at this particular time."

"Well," said Mr. Walton, "I suppose it was the motor horn eh?—what? He ought to be pretty nearly in sight around the turn by now."

Anne's shoulders straightened a little.

"Since you *have* brought it up," she said steadily, "I'd like you to finish. You didn't do it purposelessly. Do you object to a friendship between Donald Lane and myself?"

"Oh, dear me, no!" exclaimed Mr. Walton heartily. "Personally, I am delighted. Delighted! I admire the chap immensely. But—er—I can't speak for John Crane. I fancy he had his own ideas of the young man's future when he brought him out and settled him in Talimi a month or two ago; and I—er—fancy those ideas hadn't much to do with Henry Walton's daughter."

"Ah!" cried Anne quickly. "So that's it! And do you think Mr. Lane and I should carry on the family feud?"

"You could hardly call it a feud, my dear," Mr. Walton returned in mild expostulation. "I have never been a party to it, or—"

"It's a shame!" Anne interrupted. "You two men living as neighbours on the same island for I don't know how many years!"

"Twelve, my dear, as you *do* know quite well," said Mr. Walton patiently. "We settled here fourteen years ago, just after your mother died when you were a child of five, and Crane came there two years later —which, to digress, makes you nineteen now. However"—as a motor car suddenly appeared at the end of the short avenue of trees that separated the bungalow from the road—"I fancy we would better postpone any discussion on that subject for the time being."

"Or perhaps altogether," said Anne somewhat caustically. "The only answer you have ever made was that you were not a party to it."

"You are afraid it is going to be a little uncomfortable hereafter at Talimi with Donald Lane there, eh?" Mr. Walton smiled gravely. "Well, perhaps that's *the* reason why I've said what I have now, Anne."

The motor car stopped, and a broad-shouldered, dark-eyed young man, his skin tanned almost to bronze, came up the verandah steps with a quick, athletic stride, his white pith helmet in his hand.

"I'm afraid I'm late, Miss Walton," he said apologetically. "I'm frightfully sorry. Good afternoon, Mr. Walton."

"How are you, Lane?" returned Mr. Walton affably. "Glad to see you!"

"Thanks!" said Lane. He turned to the girl. "I'm not awfully late though, am I? And I've got a perfectly good excuse. The island boat's just in, and I thought I might be able to give you some news of the *Alola.* Am I forgiven?"

"You are forgiven sir," said Anne with mock gravity.

"Have a rickey, Lane?" invited Mr. Walton.

"No; thanks just the same, sir," Lane smiled. "But perhaps I'll remind you of the invitation on the way back."

"Right you are!" nodded Mr. Walton. "Well, tell us about the *Alola.* When do we get away for Talimi?"

"Just about the date we figured," Lane answered. "She's at Apia now; and Captain Croon sent word he'd be in Suva on the tenth—

that's a week from now."

"Excellent!" applauded Mr. Walton. "That's fairly close connection! Two weeks' lay-over in Suva is a lot better than usual for me."

"And in more ways than one on this occasion," Anne added; "since you dislike hotels so much."

"Yes," agreed Mr. Walton readily; "that's so! It was very decent of old Jepson to turn his bungalow over to us while he was away."

Donald Lane glanced at Anne Walton.

Anne nodded brightly in return.

"We're off, father—to nowhere in particular," she said gaily.

"Up a bit into the hills, I think," said Lane.

Mr. Walton chuckled quietly; then, with a serious note in his voice:

"I wouldn't go too far, though. I don't like the looks of the weather. The barometer's been dropping all morning like a stone shot out of a balloon, and Fiji isn't the meekest place in the world when the elements get stirred up. I remember once here in Suva when with even the houses chained down they didn't all keep their roofs on."

Lane looked incredulous.

"Literally!" said Mr. Walton. "Chains over the roofs and pegged into the ground. No foundations, of course. You haven't been out here under the Line a great while, Lane. You'll see plenty of that sort of thing if you stay long enough."

"Well," laughed Lane, "I hope I won't see any of it to-day."

"I hope not," said Mr. Walton.

The motor car drove off.

Mr. Walton resumed his seat in the reclining chair. He watched the car disappear from view, finished what remained of the contents in his tumbler, and stared for a few minutes in an absorbed sort of way at the empty glass. Then he clapped his hands smartly together.

A Fijian, in a loose white jacket and blue *lava-lava,* appeared on the verandah.

Mr. Walton motioned toward the empty glass.

It was replenished—and emptied.

Mr. Walton stared now out over the tree-tops to the distant harbour and the endless stretch of ocean beyond it. Behind the amber-lensed pince-nez his eyes had narrowed to slits, and into his face had crept a grim, almost sinister expression. Then suddenly he began to laugh.

"It was rich enough as it was," said Henry Walton. "But old Crane's nephew, too! What a hell of a joke!"

CHAPTER II   THE DELL

THE car, parked at the roadside, had been deserted for a little sylvan dell near by, through which a stream of crystal water splashed on its way down the mountain side. The wild hibiscus grew here—clusters of glorious, brilliant red against the luxuriant green of the surrounding tropical foliage. The trees arched overhead; through the interstices the sunlight came in tiny shafts, as though timorously and with diffidence to beg a role in the artistry of the cool and shady nook. Scented growth filled the air with fragrance—languorous odours, rare perfumes that invaded the senses dreamily.

Donald Lane lay on his back, his hands clasped behind his head. His eyes were fixed on Anne, who sat slightly in front of him, tossing pebbles into the stream. He could gaze his fill unobtrusively. It was just a week since he had seen her for the first time—and from that moment, it seemed, his whole life had changed. A strange thing, fate, or fortune, or chance, or whatever one chose to call it! Perhaps ridiculous, perhaps absurd—if one hadn't experienced it personally! He would have laughed at it, mocked at it himself not so very long ago. To fall in love with a girl he had never seen before, as she stood on the deck of an in-coming steamer— while he stood on the wharf, one of the crowd that always flocked there on a ship's arrival; a girl whose name even, at the time, he did not know; a girl who not only did not look at him in return, but was utterly unconscious that he existed! And yet it had been so. From that moment he had known she was the one woman in the world he wanted. He knew it in an infinitely fuller, deeper way now—after a week's companionship.

And she?

He did not know. There had been a dozen little friendly intimacies which he treasured in his favour; only he was not at all sure, the better he came to know her, but that he merely shared with every one else whom she liked and trusted that same rare and delightful charm of camaraderie which she extended so fully and ingenuously to himself.

He had not spoken to her yet. It—it took a bit of courage. Queer, that it should! He had certainly never been accused of cowardice. Why was it, then? Why was it that from time immemorial man stood abashed and tongue-tied before the maid he loved, fearing to tell her so when nothing else would daunt him? He thought he knew—now.

He had never known before. It was the hesitation, the catch of the breath, before the stakes, one's all, were risked on the answer that would open the pathway to all one hoped for, wanted, yearned for and desired—or a black nothingness, a dreary emptiness, a voided life. It was the tremor of the hand raised to knock at the portals of the Great Issue.

Anne! He had always loved the name. It seemed as though it were the one name that could have been given to her—that any other would have missed the keynote. Anne meant "grace." She seemed to symbolize that to him—and not grace only in a physical sense, but grace of mind and manner even more.

His eyes drank her in as she sat there—from the small white-shod feet and slim ankles to the finely poised head with its great coiled masses of light brown hair. In profile he could catch the oval of her face and the curve of her lips; lips that could smile adorably over the two little rows of perfect teeth; lips that—he felt his pulse quicken suddenly —he would give his all to possess. He could not see her eyes; but they were very steady, self-reliant eyes, he knew, and brown, a very wonderful shade of brown, like her hair.

She picked up the thread of their conversation without turning around; intent, apparently, on hitting a little rock in mid-stream with her pebbles.

"So Captain Croon and the *Alola* arrive on the tenth," she said. "That ought to see us in Talimi on the twelfth."

"Yes," said Lane, "if the old tub doesn't founder, or blow up, or do something else equally likely in the meantime. Croon's all right in his way, but his decrepit jitney service is at about the end of its rope, I should say."

Anne laughed.

"Yes, he's had the *Alola* as many years as I can remember. He picked her up somewhere when she was already a discarded tramp."

"For a song, so I've heard," said Lane, "though you probably know more about that than I do. And they say he's made a small fortune out of her."

"Well, he was entitled to it," Anne declared judicially. "He seized an opportunity and supplied a long-felt want—carrying supplies to the islands on a more or less regular schedule, and bringing copra and all that sort of thing back to the market, to say nothing, of course, of a passenger service as well. I think he should be ranked as a public benefactor; and, after all, the *Alola's* not so *very* uncomfortable."

"No," grinned Lane; "apart from the most hospitable tribe of cockroaches on any ship afloat, and her six knots an hour in calm weather, and Croon's idea of a menu, she's palatial! It's beastly unfortunate that the yacht's been down at Sydney for repairs and overhaul almost from the time uncle and I came out; otherwise I could have had her here, and we could all have gone back on her together and had a corking trip."

Anne made no reply.

Lane noticed that her lips drew suddenly together —she had just narrowly missed her objective with a pebble.

"Hard luck!" he encouraged cheerily. "You'll hit it next time."

There was a moment's silence.

"Do you know," said Lane slowly, "I can't get over the way we've all met here—as though it had been planned out from the very beginning of things. You come up from Auckland where you've been visiting friends; your father arrives from Europe; I'm from New York; and my uncle takes it into his head that one of the first subjects of my island-life and plantation curriculum is to come over to Suva and form the personal acquaintance of his agents and the general business community, and, incidentally, to attend to a few of his affairs—sort of a probationary expedition, I fancy. And we all meet here, each coming from a different direction."

"Well," she said, "you know what the steamship brochures say: 'Fiji—where the sea lanes meet!' I can't see anything unusual in that. People who meet for the first time have to meet somewhere, don't they?"

"Yes," said Lane, a sudden quiet in his voice, *"people* do— thousands of them, all over the world, and go on their several ways again. But I was speaking particularly of—of you and myself."

"Oh!" The exclamation escaped her in a quick and startled way. She turned around and looked at him—and was conscious of a sudden warmth in her cheeks—angrily conscious of it, because it brought confusion. He was sitting up now, leaning toward her—a big, broad-shouldered giant of a man, with dark eyes that looked very steadily into hers, and whose square, firm jaws seemed now to be curiously set and determined. She had always liked that about him—the strength and resolve in his face— it invited trust. It flashed through her mind that that had been her first impression of Donald Lane.

The pebbles dropped from her hand. Unheeded, the little shafts of sunlight that percolated through the trees faded away as though, coming to the assistance of the leafy branches, clouds high above had joined forces to repel even that small invasion of the secluded dell; unheeded, a little gust of wind came, and the red hibiscus set to nodding their heads sagely, and the gust of wind, blowing against the current, made a flurry upon the surface of the stream.

"Miss Walton"—there was a catch in Lane's voice—"I—I'm not much good at words. I brought you here this afternoon because there is something I wanted to say to you. I've wanted to say it from the moment I saw you—but you would have thought me mad. There wasn't anybody in the world but you from the time I saw you standing on the *Tofua's* deck when she docked a week ago. I— I—" He stumbled for his words, and his voice broke. Then suddenly he leaned closer to Anne and caught her hand. "I love you, Anne," he cried out hoarsely. "I love you—love you. There's just you. You've come into my life, and—and everything's all changed. Will you stay there, Anne, in my life—for always?"

She did not withdraw her hand.

"I don't know," she said—and as the words sounded in her ears she caught her breath with a little gasp. She had not meant to say that. The answer had come involuntarily, prompted by what she did not know. Not by confusion; not because she had groped blindly for something, for *anything* to say. They had come spontaneously, those words—and now they disturbed her.

He gave a low, exultant cry.

"You haven't said 'no,' Anne," he whispered. "You haven't said 'no.' "

Her eyes were on the ground, her face averted. She was trying now to understand some strange new phase in herself, something that perplexed her in an effort to be honest with herself and with this man who—who had just said he loved her. She was conscious that she liked him better at this moment than she had ever liked him before; but that was not love—was it?

Her hand was still a voluntary prisoner in his. Suddenly she looked up again, the brown eyes misty now—and suddenly, with that quick, impulsive camaraderie of hers, she laid her other hand softly across the back of his.

"I like you, Donald Lane," she said in a low voice. "I like you very, *very* much indeed; but I have never thought of you in any other way until —until now. And now"—a strange bewilderment came into her face—"I—I do not know."

"But I do!" Lane cried triumphantly. "Nothing will take you from me now. I've been too, too impetuous. I haven't given you time. But I know! And so will you— in the glorious days ahead at Talimi!"

Talimi! The word came to Anne as a shock. She had known Talimi almost as long as she could remember. She knew it far, far better than did Donald Lane, who, at best, had known it but for a few scant weeks. Not Talimi, with its beauty of lagoon and coral and the exquisite tracery of its palms against the clear moonlit sea, or its golden sunrise, or its soft breezes filled with incense that one drank in so joyously—but another side of Talimi; a sordid side; a man-made side; a side of enmity. It seemed to touch her very closely now.

She withdrew her hands quickly, and, folding them in her lap, stared at the stream.

"I am not so sure we shall see very much of each other in Talimi," she said slowly.

"Not—*what!*" he exclaimed. "Why, what do you mean?"

"Haven't you ever heard your uncle speak of us —of my father and myself?" she asked.

"No," he answered; "not otherwise than casually."

"That's strange," she said.

"Why is it strange?" he demanded. "He didn't know you were here, or that you were coming back on the *Alola.*"

"No; I suppose not." Anne spoke as though more to herself than in response to his remark.

"I don't understand!" Lane frowned in a puzzled way.

"They are not very good friends," Anne said gravely. "I—I thought you knew."

"I didn't," Lane answered quickly. "Uncle's a bit of a crusty old bachelor, of course—but his heart's right. What's the matter?"

Anne shook her head.

"I don't know," she replied a little helplessly. "It's—it's been that way for a good many years. Naturally, Mr. Crane has never confided in me— and my father won't. Fortunately, small as Talimi is, they are not often in contact with each other, for father always spends at least half of his time in Europe, and your uncle, of course, is away so much on those long cruises of his."

Lane was still frowning in a puzzled way.

"Your father hasn't shown any evidence of ill-will toward me," he said; "I mean, no sign of making it a family affair and including me in the row, whatever it is. In fact, he's been more than decent to me."

"Yes," Anne nodded; "I think he likes you tremendously. Indeed, he has said so."

"Well, then," said Lane, "that puts any presumptive interference between you and me up to my uncle."

Anne did not answer. She wondered what John Crane *would* say? She had always been fond of John Crane, and once he had been very fond of her—when she was a little girl. Everything about his plantation had been hers in those days. He had made much of her— played and frolicked with her. She remembered the time he had once made a very beautiful doll appear suddenly out of the wall of his living-room. It all came back to her now—her delight at the present, and her amazement at seeing the wall open; and then his serious warning to her to say nothing about it when, after she had made him open and shut what he called the "doll's house" several times, she had surprised him by being able to open it herself. Yes, he had been very fond of her in those old, old days. And then suddenly she had never visited John Crane's house any more—but she did not know until she was much older that the reason was because John Crane and her father were no longer friends.

"Look here," Lane cried earnestly, "don't you believe anything of that kind for a minute! Uncle's too fine an old chap for that! And, anyway, there isn't *anybody* going to interfere in this sort of thing. There's only one person can keep me from seeing as much as I want to of you in Talimi, or anywhere else—and that's Miss Anne Walton!"

Anne's face, averted, was grave and full of trouble. She could not put any answer into words because, somehow, for the first time in her life, it seemed, she was astray with her own self and impotent before an effort at self-analysis—as though she were lost in a mental maze and unable to find her way out. She did not know. That phrase seemed to have become an obsession, to crowd everything else out of her mind. What was it she did not know? Whether she loved this man or not? It was absurd! She *must* know! One couldn't help but know. Love was a matter of degree, wasn't it? One liked a person up to a certain point; and then, that line of demarcation passed, the liking became designated as the state of love. No; she wasn't even sure of that! And her silence now—what did that mean? A tacit consent—no more than that? Or a sort of pledge, a pact between them, that, whatever the attitude of others, he should see as much of her hereafter as he chose? She was conscious that he had drawn closer to her. She was in a panic-search for words—and then intervention came. A great splash of rain fell upon her hand. She stared at it for an instant in relief, almost thankfulness. Then she looked up and around her, and abruptly sprang to her feet.

"Do you hear that?" she exclaimed quickly.

There was a sound like a low moaning, a strange, eerie sound from somewhere in the far distance— then, with a rush, a great swirl of wind tore into the dell—then quiet, absolute, utter, profound; and even the patter of rain drops died away.

Lane too was on his feet.

"Yes, we're in for a bit of a thunder-shower, I think," he said. "Stay here under the shelter of the trees while I trot out to the car and get the top up."

Anne glanced at him, her lips suddenly tight— and, seizing his arm, began to run toward the road.

"Don't wait to put any top up!" she cried. "There isn't an instant to lose; and, besides, it would either be blown to ribbons itself or blow the car over. You've got to drive, and drive like mad —while there's a road."

"You mean—" His words were swept away in another sudden onrush of wind.

She nodded her head quickly.

"My God," he jerked out, "it's growing as black as night!"

CHAPTER III   THE STORM

SOMEWHERE, a tree, uprooted, crashed and fell to the ground—and the sound, out of the great swelter of discordant sounds, was like the snapping of a little twig.

Hands clasping where they might, clinging with all her strength to hold herself in her seat, Anne sat white-faced, and, save for the vicious slew and lurch of the car, immovable.

She could scarcely see beyond the hood of the car. The whole world seemed to have turned into a weird, ugly, dark-brown coloured dusk. Driven with terrific force by the wind, the rain came in deluge after deluge. The flooring of the car at moments was awash with it; it was as though water in illimitable volume were being hurled and hurled against the windshield.

Rocking, careening, the car raced on down the mountain side; and the road, cut through the thick forest, was a winding, twisting canon of storm—as if the elements, impatient at anything that impeded their progress, had seized upon this narrow ribbon of open, man-made space along which to vent their violence unrestrained and to the full.

Roll on roll of thunder, that the wind mocked as a puny competitor to its own malignant screaming, came through the wrack of tempest as a minor note —like subdued, intermittent murmurings suggestive of sullen discontent. Flashes of lightning, meteor streaks that brought hurt to the eyeballs, so close they were, seemed to stab again and again at the car itself; seemed to have picked it out as a wriggling, squirming thing that, in its mad, unhinged race for life, was first to be tormented in malicious glee before it was at last, when the sport tired, contemptuously snuffed out and flung aside.

Anne's eyes were half closed. She was not conscious of fear; she was conscious only of a strange, calm wonder whether there was an even chance of getting through or not.

"The barometer has been falling all morning like a stone dropped from a balloon."

Her father's words came back to her. They *had* gone too far—no, that wasn't it. This would never have caught them if it hadn't been for that little dell whose leafy roof had shut out the signs of warning that, out in the open, they would have had in plenty of time.

She remembered a hurricane that had once swept Talimi. That

was long ago—when she was a child, ten years old. It was very vivid still in her mind— horribly vivid—great areas where trees had been mown down as though a giant sickle had been at work; and houses and native huts had been destroyed as utterly as though they had been so many stacks of loosely piled hay.

How much farther had they to go before they could find shelter? Shelter! What constituted shelter? In the main storm track—nothing! It was getting worse every minute. Perhaps this wasn't a hurricane— perhaps it was just a cloudburst, or a very severe wind and rain storm. That would account for the barometer. But they would never be able to get as far as the bungalow anyway. The road already was turning into a watercourse, its bed a mass of liquid mud upon which the car was skidding perilously. No; it wasn't that alone—it was the wind. The car seemed to be literally blown along and flipped like a straw from side to side.

There was a house, she thought, not far from here—if it were still standing—the Robertson place. But she wasn't quite sure where she was now. It was hard to tell—hard to see. It was getting darker than it had been. The brownish murk was edging into a strange purple. Perhaps the best thing to do would be to get out and stay in the woods.

The car seemed suddenly to acquire greater velocity and be borne along in a mighty dive. She heard a sound now—a sound that would not be denied by the wild shrieking of the wind—a crash, a rip and tear and split of falling timber. She saw something go down beside her at the edge of the road —a mass of trees. Shelter in the woods! She laughed a little hysterically.

She looked at the man beside her. His clothes were sodden—like a thin plaster on his back—and, as he crouched forward over the wheel, exerting, it seemed, every ounce of strength that he possessed, she could see the play of the great muscles across his shoulders. She saw his face. It was set like iron, the jaws clamped and rigid; but dominant in it was a grim fearlessness—that unbeaten something that survives destruction itself.

He turned his head suddenly toward her for an instant—and shouted something.

She understood; not his words—she could not have heard him if he had placed a megaphone to her ear. The car was out of control. He was working madly with the mechanism. The mud made a greased runway of the road; the wheels would not hold. They probably were not even touching the ground. The car seemed to be bodily lifted as though the wind, to be balked no longer, had at last got a purchase beneath it. It brought flashing through her mind again one of those child pictures of that day in Talimi. It had looked like an enormous, grotesque and uncouth bird soaring through the sky. As a child, it had seemed to her to be some new and terrifying monster of the air. It had been a shed on the plantation.

In the murk, the semi-darkness, the grey, drab curtain of lashing rain, the sense of sight telegraphed but a vague impression to the brain—the brain painted in the details. Something that gave the impression of a huge club wielded by invisible and gigantic hands, but which she knew to be an uprooted tree, struck at the motor's hood—and missed—and lay a few feet ahead athwart the car's path. It was the end. Something whispered that within her. It did not frighten her. She had simply the numbed understanding that the disaster which was inevitable was to take this form.

And then suddenly she saw the great shoulders beside her heave themselves free of the wheel, and she was conscious that Donald Lane had interposed his body between her and what must be the direction of the impact, and that his arms were around her.

There was a terrific crash, a shock, a strange recoil—then momentary oblivion. And then out of nothingness there came a sense of chaos, twisted debris, a sprawled car, tree branches—and a motionless form beneath her, yielding, soft, as though still to shield her, a face, terribly white and rigid, with closed eyes.

A great cry came from her. Madly she struggled to her knees.

"Donald! Donald! Donald!" she cried over and over again. A surge of terror, of anguish such as she had never known before possessed her. And in that instant her heart was naked for her to gaze upon through blinding tears. This man was *her* man—and he always, always had been; from all time he had been. But she only knew it now when it was perhaps too late, for he was so still that she was afraid— afraid that he was dead. She raised his head—it was bleeding profusely. "Donald! Donald!" she cried out again pitifully. "I know now! I know now! Donald, I *do* love you—you are all the world to me. Don't you hear me, Donald? You asked me if I cared. Oh, in God's pity, speak to me!"

There was no answer—no movement.

Dead! She covered her face with her hands and moaned like a child. There was no storm, no wild dismay of battling elements—only the grief, the agony, the awful turmoil, the abysmal sense of loss in her own soul—a faltering prayer.

And then she staggered to her feet and with all her strength strove to drag the inert form free of the wreckage. She could not move him. Tree and car and branches were all entangled together. But she thought that he had stirred—slightly—so slightly that she was afraid to harbour it as true.

She threw herself down beside him again—and then, with a low, glad cry, began to tear her white underskirt into strips, and staunch the flow of blood about the temples, and wrap a bandage around his head. He wasn't dead! He wasn't dead! She said that to herself again and again.

Somehow she managed to drag one of the cushioned seats from the car, and somehow get it under his head and shoulders.

But there was no sign of returning consciousness. His heart was beating faintly; she could detect that—but nothing more. She was dry-eyed now, her face pinched and haggard and deathly pale. She bent and kissed him, kissed the closed eyes and his lips, holding his face tenderly between her two hands.

"I—I won't be long, Donald," she whispered brokenly. "I—I'll come back—and—and—oh, wait for me, Donald!"

She must get help, and get it quickly—very quickly. That was the only chance. She scrambled over the car, and tore her way through the entangling branches. The Robertsons' house—there wasn't any other place! She didn't know how near that was; but, near or far, she must reach it. She was only sure that they had not passed it as yet on the way down.

The wind half swept her from her feet, blew her along, wrapped her soaked skirts about her until they manacled her limbs, and she staggered and caught at a tree-trunk at the side of the road to save herself from falling. Her hair, loosened, dripping wet, streamed about her shoulders, and, in the wind, strands of it whipped her face. She raised her hands to brush it away from her eyes—and gave a sharp, sudden cry of pain. Her left arm hurt her brutally. She had not noticed that before. And there was something warm—much warmer than the rain—upon her cheeks. She looked at her hands— they were red with it as they came away from her face.

She moaned a little; she felt suddenly giddy and weak—and then something, a tigerish something rose within her, and she stumbled on again. She was being robbed of a priceless treasure; this ghastly chaos that was all around her was trying to steal from her the love that she had just found. But nothing would steal that from her; nothing would rob her of that! She would fight for it until she died; she would never yield it up—never—never yield it up to either man or storm, or for any cause, now that she had found it. It was hers—hers forever—a wonderful, wonderful thing. Love! Yes, yes; she loved—with every fibre of her being, with every breath, with every thought!

Her mind grew strangely confused.

"Blooey!" The word kept repeating itself. What did "blooey" mean? Where had she heard it? What a hideous, hideous word!

He mustn't die—his life depended upon her. He shouldn't die—she wouldn't let him. He wouldn't die—she was sure of that—her soul bade her believe it if only she could win her way through. And she would win her way through—she must—she *would* win her way through!

She struggled on—but more and more blindly at every yard. At times she was literally blown forward, and flung either to her face in the road or against the trees that, still standing, bent their heads like bows to the wind; at times she crawled on hands and knees, clawing with bitter pain for every inch. She became as one who had lost all human semblance; her clothing torn to shreds; her eyes, with feverish, unnatural brilliancy, burning out through a mass of matted and mud-caked hair.

On and on she went—like an animal sorely hurt, crying out at times, making strange, pitiful sounds.

Coherent thought was battered out of her; her mind like her body was bruised and bleeding. Instinct alone remained.

And then at last she beat with her fists upon the panels of a door; and the door was opened a few inches against the storm.

"Great God!" a man's voice bellowed out.

She seized his hand, plucked at his sleeve, trying to pull him out through the doorway.

"Come! Come quickly!" she cried. "Up the road—Donald Lane—under the car. Come— *come!*" she urged deliriously; and, turning, took a step forward to start back again—and collapsed, a huddled, unconscious heap, upon the ground.

CHAPTER IV   THE MIDNIGHT VISITOR

THE moonlight streamed in through the window and lay soft and filmy white upon the appointments of the room. The night was very lovely —a tropical night of serene and glorious beauty. From her bed, Anne could look outside to where, bathed in the moon rays, verdure and foliage took on the most wonderful and delicate shades and colourings. And it was very quiet—very still. Not a leaf on the top of a tall palm that was directly in line with the window and that she had been watching for ever so long, moved, apparently, by the slightest fraction of an inch.

She could not sleep; she did not know that she even wished to sleep—the morrow was filled with the promise of so much happiness and glad excitement. Sleep had not come; but dreams had very happy dreams, dreams that were full of tender fancies, dreams that changed all the world as she had known it before into one of such new wonder that, as she caught glimpses of it, it brought an eager burning into her cheeks and made her heart to beat the faster. There was no one to see; no one to know—only the still night dreaming itself in the moonlight. Almost subconsciously she heard the clock in the bungalow now strike midnight.

Oh, there was so much! The *Alola* had come in that afternoon from Apia, and would sail to-morrow evening for Talimi. And to-morrow, for the first time since that terrible day, she would see Donald Lane again.

She had been ill; quite ill, they had told her. For several days she had remembered nothing of what had happened. Indeed, yesterday was the first time she had been allowed to walk a little on the verandah; but to-day she had been splendid, really herself again she felt, though the doctor had still ordered quiet and had been very stingy about exercise or excitement of any kind. She had intended to drive down to Suva to—to—well, she had *said* there were a number of things she needed before leaving for Talimi. The doctor's refusal had been more emphatic than elegant—but the disappointment was compensated for by the note which he had taken from his pocket and handed her.

A little smile crept across her lips; a little tinge of colour stole into her cheeks. The doctor was really a dear. She had had first-hand information about Donald everyday. Donald! It was always "Donald" in her thoughts. The colour deepened. She wondered if she dared—to say it aloud. Donald! It—it was quite different to say it in one's thoughts, or cry it out in the wild abandon of grief and fear as she had done in the storm when he had lain so still. She half buried her face in the pillow —and gave a little catch of her breath.

"Donald!" she whispered in a small, timid voice —and then suddenly came courage born of impulse out of her soul. "Oh, Donald, dear, I do love you!" she breathed. "I love you so much! How could I ever have thought I did not know, when I must have cared all the time just as I care now! But I think you know now, dear—I—I hope you do —I—I wonder if you do?"

Did he? Her heart was beating very quickly. Could he read between the lines of her note sent in answer to his that the doctor had brought her? She had not been unmaidenly—she would rather have died than that. But surely he would understand. They had not seen each other since the accident. When the storm was over, Donald had been taken to the hotel in Suva, and she had been brought back here to the bungalow. And for a week they had both been invalids. She remembered the great throb of joy that had welled up in her heart when they had told her he was not dangerously hurt, or even, in a sense, seriously so— "rather badly cut up and a number of severe contusions, but no bones broken—constitution of a horse, matter of a week," the doctor had said.

Flowers! Her room was full of his flowers.

And then his note to-day which she had answered. She could repeat every word of it. It had begun *most* informally! She smiled a little in happy understanding over that. He had hesitated at "Anne;" and he had refused flatly the conventional "Miss Walton"—so just nothing at all!

"I'll look less like a turbaned East Indian with the bandages off my head to-morrow. Am going up to call for you at the bungalow to bring you down to the *Alola*—may I?

Donald Lane."

And she had said in reply that—oh, what *had* she said! Her cheeks grew suddenly crimson. But she was glad—glad—glad! That reference to Talimi which, in view of what he had said about those days to come, he could not possibly misunderstand! She would not have retracted it now for worlds. Was he happy to-night, as happy as she was? Was he dreaming to-night—dreaming awake as she was—of to-morrow, the wonderful to-morrow?

John Crane—Talimi! A little frown gathered on her brow. Was that going to be a source of unpleasantness? Surely not! Fortunately her father had already expressed himself; but even if he hadn't she knew that, though it would cause her sorrow and mar her happiness to oppose her father, her love for Donald came first now, above all things else—now and for always and always. But why should she think only of that side? There was another side. Perhaps this love that had come to Donald and herself would be the one thing that would bring John Crane and her father together again after all these years. That was the way she wanted it to be—what she would work to bring about. Of course, she would succeed! Her father was already won over, and—

She sat suddenly upright in bed. Fancy? Well, it had been most strangely realistic, then! It had seemed as though a shadow had flitted across the moon path there outside the window—not a waving branch, or anything of that kind, because there wasn't a breeze strong enough to stir even a leaf— but a shadow, come and gone in an instant, that, in the momentary glimpse she had caught of it, had looked like a man passing swiftly by.

She listened intently. There was not a sound. But, then, there wouldn't necessarily be any sound. One could walk out there on the grass in absolute silence. Yet, on the other hand, who could possibly be out there at this hour? It was long after midnight. It *must* be fancy—it couldn't be anything else. No one would be prowling around at this time of night way up here in the hills—not even a native. But it hadn't looked like a native; the impression was very vivid—it had looked like a white man.

Anne pursed her lips. Hadn't she already decided it was merely fancy? Well, perhaps she had; but she wasn't satisfied. It wasn't her father because he had retired long before she had—and there wasn't anybody else here except the native servants.

Still she listened. A minute that spent itself in a thumping, palpitating silence dragged by—and then Anne quickly and silently sprang from her bed. The sound was very faint—but it was not fancy. Some one had moved stealthily across the verandah, and some one was now *trying* the front door.

And somehow it made her suddenly think of that night in Paris at

Mère Gigot's—perhaps it was the suggestion of *stealth* that was responsible for this swift veering trend of her thoughts. In any case it was not voluntary! She had tried to forget that night. Now it suddenly rose up before her . . . the wounded man in the lane . . . Mère Gigot . . . . the sordid wine-cellar, with its still more sordid and depraved *habitues* . . . Fire-Eyes . . . She had never heard any more of, or from, any of them. She had told her father about it, of course, and her father had seized upon that episode to point out to her how fully it warranted his disapproval of her work amongst the city's slums. Neither of them had mentioned the subject again. Her father, in view of the fact that no unpleasant consequences had developed, had been content to let the matter drop; she, on her part, had striven her utmost to forget it. It was not a pleasant memory. There had been something of ugly menace, something of evil stealth about that whole night, just as there now was about this shadowy thing that, a moment ago, had sped past her window and had moved furtively along the verandah to the front door.

And now she was not sure, but she thought she heard the front door being cautiously opened. That was strange—very strange indeed! The door was invariably locked at night. Her father always made a point of seeing to that before retiring.

She flung a dressing-gown over her shoulders, and from a drawer of her dresser took out a revolver. She was conscious of agitation, and this sudden and swift flash of memory conjuring up the most fearsome experience she had ever known was not reassuring, but it in no way affected her actions—she had lived too much of her life in the open places of the world, where self-reliance and self-dependence were the first essentials of even ordinary comfort, to know either flurry or hesitation now, any more than she had permitted such feelings to sway her in the lane that night in Paris with the wounded Englishman.

Her father's rooms opened off the entrance hall of the bungalow, but on the opposite side from those which she occupied. She would, therefore, have to cross the hall, and, incidentally, the line of the front door before she could reach him. There was not another soul in the bungalow—the servants all had their quarters outside and at the rear.

The door of her bedroom, leading into a sort of little boudoir and sitting-room beyond, was open, and silently, her bare feet making no sound on the mat-covered floorings, she crossed the two rooms to the farther door of the sitting-room, which, closed now, gave directly on the wide entrance hall itself.

And here she paused for an instant, and once more listened. There was undoubtedly the sound of movement again, guarded, cautious, and from *inside* the bungalow now. Anne's lips drew very tightly together. She was quite cool, quite resolute; her contact with, oftentimes, the rougher, cruder element, the driftwood of humanity that swarmed the tropics, had taught her to face emergency of any sort without flinching, but it had never taught her to be anything but a woman, with all the more sensitive tendencies of her sex—her heart was pounding furiously. She did not like this present situation, she did not like it at all; but the idea of retreating from it was the last thing that would have entered her head. She possessed exactly that sort of courage—the sort to carry on. She was not fearless—very far from it; but she never allowed fear to become her master.

She opened the sitting-room door softly—and peered out into the entrance hall. On either side of the front door was a window, and through these windows the moonlight streamed into the hall just as it did into her bedroom. She could see almost as well as though it were day. There was no one in sight—the hall was empty of any intruder.

And then, on the instant, Anne's dark eyes opened wide. There was a light in her father's room just across the hall—it showed like a thin, yellow thread along his door-sill. She smiled a little in sudden relief. The bogey she had conjured up was her father. And then, quite as suddenly, she caught her breath a little in anxiety. Why should he get up at this hour and go to the front door, go out on the verandah, go outside the house? Perhaps he was ill and had not wanted to disturb her? No, that would hardly account for it—but something, at any rate, must be the matter.

She crossed the hall quickly, and, with her hand half raised to knock upon the door, let it fall again to her side. He wasn't alone. Some one was in there with him. She could hear voices now—her father's, and that of another man. They came to her in a muffled way, but she could catch the words without difficulty. It was rather strange—a rather strange hour for a visitor! But it was her father's affair. She certainly had no right to intrude. It was very peculiar, though! She couldn't understand. It would seem almost as though her father had been *expecting* his visitor. It must have been her father she had heard at the front door—unlocking it.

She half turned away—and abruptly stood still again. Words came throbbing through her brain, words in her father's voice. They seemed to paralyze her very power of movement, to root her to the spot:

"John Crane, the old swine, will never know he's been done until you've had a chance to put the globe between you half a dozen times over if you want to."

Another voice spoke:

"Well, I'm not worrying; though, according to your own account, the old chap's a tough bird to monkey with if his tail's pulled—and I'd say that separating him from a package of jewels worth a hundred thousand pounds is pulling his tail *some!*"

"The only trouble you're likely to have with him," said Mr. Walton with a malicious laugh, "is getting away from his damned hospitality so as to get over to my place and split the swag before the *Alola* sails again. He'll hand over the package the minute you show him the list in his handwriting, and then fall on your neck and slobber over you like a long-lost son."

"Right, you are!" The other echoed Mr. Walton's malicious laugh. "Well, let's get down to business. I've steered clear of you here in Suva until the last minute. Is everything still safe, and the coast clear for me to go aboard the *Alola* tomorrow? Nothing's cropped up to put a crimp in anywhere?"

"Nothing!" Mr. Walton answered. "Everything is all right. And I've found out about Solly Minderlich in Bombay. He's safe enough, and you can cash in your share with him, if you want to, without fear of police interference—but he'll screw the eye teeth out of you."

"Will he!" ejaculated the other. "Then he'll be pretty good if he does—he, or any other man of his kidney! I'll take care of anything like that he—"

Anne moved blindly away from the door. Her head was whirling. This was unbelievable—it couldn't be true. It was preposterous— ridiculous —absurd. Only there was an ache, a horrible agony in her brain. She put her hands up before her eyes, and pressed them fiercely against her temples. A thief! Her father was going to steal —steal jewels worth a hundred thousand pounds from John Crane.

She was walking across the hall, scarcely conscious of her movements; walking automatically— subconsciously seeking her own room. There was a small wicker table in the centre of the hall.

She did not see it. It fell to the floor as she stumbled into it.

Mechanically she stooped and righted the table.

On the floor where they had fallen were a number of magazines and papers, and a checkered cap, which, since it did not belong to her father, obviously belonged to his visitor—and mechanically, too, she picked these things up and replaced them on the table.

Her father's door had opened. He stood outside it now holding a lamp in one hand; with his other hand he had closed the door so that she caught no glimpse of the interior.

"You, Anne!" he exclaimed.

"Yes," she said.

He came a step forward, and raised the lamp so that its rays fell upon her.

Her face was white, haggard, with no single vistage of colour in it.

"Oh!" said Mr. Walton without inflection in his voice. "You've been listening?"

"I heard what was said," she answered dully.

Henry Walton's lips curved slowly into a smile— a very cool and composed little smile—a very deadly little smile. But no other muscle of his face moved.

"My dear," he said softly, "if you will excuse me for a few moments, I will join you presently in your room."

Anne made no attempt to reply.

The door of Mr. Walton's room opened just sufficiently to admit him—and closed behind him again.

CHAPTER V   THE PACT

IF the man who had been in her father's room had left the bungalow, it had been without Anne's knowledge. She had not heard any one go out. But then it might very well have been that she was far too absorbed, in far too great mental distress, to have paid any attention, even if the man had slammed the front door behind him. She stood now beside the table in her sitting-room, a rigid little figure with hands clenched at her sides, as Henry Walton entered and set the lamp which he carried down between them.

Anne did not look up, though she was quite well aware that her father was regarding her fixedly. She was still fighting for mental composure, for her very reason itself, it seemed—as she had been fighting from that moment out there in the hall which seemed ages and ages ago, so long ago that all her old life with its buoyancy, its gladness, it hopes, its joys of living, had passed away, and in its place had come a new existence, foreign, incomprehensible and abhorrent to her. Her mind could not grasp it except in broken fragments, could not somehow piece those fragments together, could not correlate them—they remained fragments.

"My dear," said Mr. Walton in smooth and perfectly modulated tones, "you should really make an effort to control your facial expression if you care anything about the privacy of your thoughts. Shall I tell you what you are thinking? It is rather jumbled, isn't it? You are dazed; shame touches you because you are the daughter of one who plots a criminal act; your pride is badly hurt; and you have not yet got to the stage of weighing with any degree of nicety the effect this will have on your filial devotion. At one moment, prompted more by selfishness than a high sense of morality, you rebel like a spoilt child against having heard what you did, since otherwise, though the crime might be consummated, it would leave your conscience untouched; the next moment, the fact that you *do* know brings a gleam of hope since you imagine this thing will thereby be nipped in the bud, and, though a bit tattered and with a rent or two in it, you can still wrap some sort of a mantle of self-respect around yourself; and lastly, but perhaps most disturbing of all, always hovering in the background when it is not to the fore, embracing in a most confusing way all the emotion that flesh is heir to, and involving the past, the present and the future, is the thought of— Donald Lane."

78

She shivered a little—not merely because he had so mercilessly expressed her thoughts in words, but because of his ruthless, impersonal tones, his suave casualness, his utter lack of any display of feeling. She looked up at him now for the first time—and suddenly, as though she had received a shock, drew back from the table. She was conscious that there was something different in his appearance, that he did not look the same as usual. He was not wearing the amber-coloured pince-nez! That was what it was! The thick, amber-coloured lenses, that she had heard him so often explain to his friends in Paris were worn because his long residence in the tropics had permanently injured his optic nerves, toned down the intense and otherwise instantly noticeable brilliancy of his eyes, and produced the soft and almost slumbrous appearance to which she was accustomed. In all her life, even as a child, she could never remember having seen him without his amber-coloured glasses until now. She could never remember, for instance, now that she looked back, ever having seen him perform so common and natural an act as to take them off to polish them in her presence. And now the effect without them was so startling and forbidding that something chill and ominous clutched suddenly at her heart stilling its beat.

And she stood grasping at her chair, the colour fleeing from her cheeks, staring at him. His eyes bored into her. They were unforgettable eyes as they held her in focus now. They seemed to snap fire from their jet-black depths, to grow and grow in size, to burn through and through her. There were no other eyes like these in all the world—and yet she had seen a pair of eyes *identical* with these before. But there was no black beard now, and no cloak. But the eyes—she could never forget them, never mistake them. *Unless she were mad!* Perhaps she was mad. But something else came back to her now, like a pointing finger in its significance. That momentary faltering of those eyes as they had met hers in Mère Gigot's that night, the quick, startled, muscular contraction of the man's lips, gone as swiftly as it had come, when he and she had stood face to face in that abominable place. She had thought it imagination then on her part—she knew now, and horror held her in its grip, that his self-possession, marvellous as it might be, had been shaken for an instant as he had recognized her, his *daughter,* there.

"Fire-Eyes!" she screamed out suddenly—and covered her face with her hands.

"Really, my dear," said Mr. Walton suavely, "it is amazing that you should recognize me—since I left off my glasses for that purpose. I propose to hide nothing from you. How could I, if we are to exchange confidences—which I am afraid we will now be obliged to do for—er—our our mutual welfare. That was a charming little evening at the incomparable Gigot's wasn't it?—but" —as Anne moaned suddenly— "we will not refer to it, my dear, unnecessarily. So will you begin, Anne, by telling me what you heard from the other side of my door? I judged from that very impressionable countenance of yours that you heard pretty much everything."

Anne drew herself erect with an effort; her voice sounded hollow in her own ears; her mouth was strangely dry.

"I heard you plotting to rob John Crane of some valuable jewels in Talimi," she said. "I heard enough to make me believe then that my father was a potential thief—but—now I know he—he is far worse than that. That he is—"

"A professional criminal, Anne," supplied Mr. Walton gently. "Quite so, my dear. I have been a criminal all my life. It is well that you understand now at the beginning, so that you can exclude from your mind any idea that the present venture is some new experience in life from which I may still be dissuaded, and—er—saved."

"All—all your life?" The words came from Anne in a numbed way.

"Quite all my life," nodded Mr. Walton. "And I might say, with one exception, very successfully so; in fact, I am not sure that I should admit an exception, for, indeed, thanks to that incident, the police of several continents no longer search for one that they are perfectly certain has been dead for many years. And I might also say, Anne, that I am neither unmindful of, nor ungrateful for, the assistance that you, quite unwittingly of course, have been to me in preserving my incognito. You have—er—contributed just that air of respectability to my modest establishments both in Paris and Talimi that locks the door upon suspicion."

She stared at him for an instant, a look in her eyes like that of a wounded animal; then she sank into her chair, and buried her face in her hands.

Something cataclysmic seemed to have taken place in her life—something that had torn violently and suddenly asunder every bond that had once united her to all she had ever known of friends, of companionship, and even of environment. "All his life," he had said. Her father was a professional criminal. He was worse even that that. He was a murderer. Madame Frigon had said so. It burned into her brain, searing her with its frightful brand, proclaiming her an outcast and a pariah from all she cared for. She was the daughter of a criminal and a murderer. All she cared for! She cared for Donald Lane—but— she was the daughter of a criminal—and—and a criminal's daughter and Donald Lane lived in two different worlds.

A question came involuntarily to her lips.

"Did—did my mother know you for what you are?" she asked.

Henry Walton smiled faintly.

"I rather expected the question," he said quietly. "No, she never knew I was a criminal."

"Thank God for that!" whispered Anne.

"Yes," he said; "it was perhaps just as well!"

Anne moaned a little, her face still buried in her hands. His callousness was horrible. She knew what he was—she had seen him in his criminal surroundings, and in his role of Fire-Eyes when he stood out as an acknowledged leader even among the most abandoned and evil of the Paris underworld, she had seen him commit an act that only a fiend would commit; but she didn't want to believe it, fought against believing it, because, if it were true, her own life, in the sense of everything that made life worth while to her, was at an end. How could it be true? His life here in the islands, his hosts of friends— everybody knew Henry Walton and liked him! Hadn't Mr. Jepson, for instance, who was a gentleman of the highest standing, insisted on turning over his very bungalow here to his friend "Henry?" And the circle of "nice people" in Paris! It was incredible!

He seemed to read her thoughts with uncanny precision.

"That is the art of it, my dear," he said smoothly. "It makes my position unassailable. Besides being extremely fond of the life out here—during certain periods of the year!—the little plantation on Talimi serves, when I am in Paris, to account to the Parisians for the source of my income; and, when I am out here, those who know there is scarcely a livelihood to be made out of the plantation do not for an instant question the fact that I have additional investments in Europe. A most admirable arrangement that not only allows me to indulge my rather diverse tastes in respect of climate, but serves my interests to perfection!"

Something in Anne's throat seemed to choke her. She knew a sudden rush of passion. His callousness, a sort of inhuman, perverted facetiousness in both his voice and manner had robbed her of even a feeling of *tolerance* toward him, which otherwise might naturally, in spite of abhorrence for all he was and all he stood for, have arisen from their relationship one to the other. With every word he uttered, he seemed to glory in his shame and boast about it—a shame that was her shame, too, now.

"You have said enough!" she cried. "I know you now for what you are. I have seen you at your work. I have heard tales of you that are enough to make one's blood run cold. And I understand now that I have lived all my life in more or less luxury— on stolen money. I do not know how much you have stolen, how many times, or when, or where, but you have robbed me of more than you have robbed all others in all your life."

"Strange!" murmured Henry Walton. "The fundamental selfishness of human nature—even, as I have said, as applied to one's morality! As between father and daughter, you appear to have eliminated every thought—except for the daughter."

Anne's small hands clenched.

"Do you expect me to rejoice in your dishonest life?" she burst out passionately. "Do you expect me, because you are my father, to become a criminal, too—or even to countenance your acts—or—or—" Her voice broke. She turned away her head for a moment. "You have said enough!" She steadied her voice. "You have warned me that you are past reformation. I do not know what I shall do in the future, I—I can't think now; but at least this projected robbery from Mr. Crane will never take place."

"We are coming to that," said Henry Walton calmly. "I can't say I am at all surprised at your attitude; and it is precisely because I anticipated that attitude that I am so frank with you. My dear, I regret to say that, however distasteful it may be to you, our arrangements and plans in regard to John Crane and his seductive jewels are too complicated and—er—conclusive to allow of any change being made in them."

Anne's lips straightened.

"You will never touch one of them while I live!" she said steadily.

"The optimism of youth!" Henry Walton smiled blandly. "It sees so little of the way ahead! But do not let us be hasty, Anne. You say that I have already said enough; I am afraid that I have still more to say. Except for that memorable evening at Mère Gigot's when you did not of course recognize me, due to a perhaps pardonable resort to the somewhat melodramatic disguise in the shape of a beard and cloak which I affect for obvious reasons on such occasions, you have never seen me as I am to-night—like this." He touched his eyes lightly with his fingers. "In spite of the years and the abundant evidence of my death, there are still those to-day, in the Prefecture of Paris, in the hallowed precincts of Scotland Yard, and elsewhere, who would not hesitate long, I fancy, to lay a hand upon my shoulder if they saw me as you see me now. My eyes, in certain respects, were always a curse to me—when they were not a blessing! You are a woman of common sense, my dear—of unusual common sense. What I have shown you and what I have said is merely by way of bringing home to you the fact that my plans will permit of no interference—*from any one*—at any cost. I shall go farther along those same lines— and for the same purpose. I shall tell you about John Crane's jewels, and exactly how I propose to get them; and I hope for your sake it will then at once become fully obvious to you that with my—er —I think I might almost say quite literally, my life—in the hollow of your hand, there is no alternative but that of force if you refuse to agree to the proposition I shall make to you."

Anne stared at him wildly.

"I think you are mad—or I am!" she cried out. "Your 'proposition' is an insult before you make it. There is nothing you can say or do that will prevent me from stopping this thing if you attempt to go on with it."

"We will see," said Henry Walton coolly. "Broken waters, my dear, sometimes interfere with the course we propose to steer. Will you permit me to finish?"

Anne did not answer.

"Briefly," said Henry Walton, ignoring her silence, "a man by the name of Martin Todd, who is an old friend of John Crane, aided a little group of the Russian nobility to escape from their country, and, incidentally, succeeded in salvaging for them at the same time a very choice collection of jewels—very choice, my dear Anne—to the estimated value, as you may have heard when you stood outside my door, of some hundred thousand pounds, or, as your friend Mr.

Donald Lane of New York would say, a cool half million. The Soviet Government, however, had their agents hot on the trail of these jewels, and both the refugees and Todd himself were being watched in Paris. The jewels were securely hidden, but they were also useless, while hidden, to people in dire need of exchanging at least a portion of them for cash; ergo, they must be got away secretly out of the country to some place where, with the Soviet agents thrown off the scent, they could be turned into money. John Crane was at Havre with his yacht. Todd sent the jewels to Crane, and Crane agreed to take them to Talimi. The jewels were to be redeemed in person either by Todd, or the man who had acted as Todd's messenger, or, as Crane did not know any of the refugees personally, by whichever one of the latter who identified himself by presenting a copy of the list, in Crane's own handwriting, of the articles the package contains and the names of those to whom each separate article belongs. One of these latter, one of these ex-Russian noblemen, to be precise, is on his way now to reclaim the jewels; is, in fact, in Suva at the present moment, and will be on board the *Alola* to-morrow en route for Talimi. I need hardly explain, my dear, that he will not reach Talimi with the credentials in his pocket, and that *some one else* will present them."

Amazement, as Anne listened, crowded out for the moment all other emotions.

"It seems a very strange coincidence that out of all the world the little island of Talimi should be involved in this, and that you, who live there, should know of it!" she exclaimed abruptly. "How do you know that all this is so? How *could* you know?"

"My dear," replied Henry Walton, a slightly wearied tone creeping into his voice, "life itself is merely a succession of coincidences—like a row of beads strung on a thread. The most commonplace happenings are coincidences, you will find, if you only stop to analyze them. As to how I know about this, it is my business—er—profession to know about such things whenever possible. We have perfected in Paris a very efficient organization. The Soviet agents were a bit clumsy; they supplied us with our first clue— after that, Todd and his band of exiles were not so secret in their councils as they fondly imagined they were. The rest required only patience. Crane had sailed back to Talimi; it was simply a question of who had the credentials—" He paused—and a grimly amused smile touched his lips. "I wonder if you knew who had them? I wonder if you remember by any chance a man named Kendall who—er—introduced you to Mère Gigot?"

Anne started violently. Kendall—the wounded Englishman! Yes, she remembered now. The Russians—Kendall's reference to the Soviet agents —that *letter* whose address he was willing to risk even his life to keep secret—the letter that, at any cost, he had insisted on posting with his own hand.

"Kendall!" she cried out. "You can't mean that it is Kendall you are following, that it is Kendall who will be aboard the *Alola* to-morrow, for Kendall is an Englishman."

Henry Walton shook his head.

"Oh, no," he said. "Not Kendall—for Kendall, though I have no doubt he is doing well, is still at least a semi-invalid from his wound. Not Kendall, my dear—but the man to whom Kendall posted the letter you told us about so dramatically that night —one of the band of refugees, to repeat what I said a moment ago, one of the ex-Russian noblemen. The 'letter,' as you have no doubt already surmised, contained the credentials."

"But the address!" Anne's hands were clasped to her temples. Her head was throbbing brutally. "No one knew that—no one but Kendall."

"No, my dear Anne," purred Henry Walton. "You are quite wrong. *I* knew it. Kendall told me."

"Kendall told you!" Anne exclaimed. "But—but I—"

"He became slightly delirious after you left us." Mr. Walton shrugged his shoulders. "And, as so often happens in such cases, he had an obsession. His obsession was that address—he repeated it, over and over, at least a dozen times."

Anne made no comment.

"The man to whom Kendall sent the credentials suddenly left Paris," continued Mr. Walton. "That put the Soviet agents out of the running. They did not know the man's ultimate destination—and we did. We followed, caught up with the man en-route—and to-morrow we begin the last lap of the journey."

"Which"—Anne spoke dully—"you say he will not finish?"

"Exactly!" said Henry Walton.

"You—you have let him come this far without interference?" Anne's mind was confused.

"Except to assure ourselves that he carried the credentials and *where* he carried them—yes," Henry Walton answered, and now an ominous little smile touched his lips. "That perplexes you? The explanation is simple. We are not children. When we leave Suva there is neither wireless nor cable communication; up to that point there is. It would really have been an unpardonable blunder to have risked the emissary's misadventure coming to the ears of his fellows while there was still a chance for them to embarrass us."

Anne rose suddenly to her feet.

"This is horrible!" she cried out. "It is monstrous! Inhuman! What are you going to do with this man—to keep him from reaching Talimi after he is on board the *Alola?*"

Henry Walton shrugged his shoulders.

"That is rather immaterial, isn't it?" he returned indifferently. "Accidents are of so many and diverse a nature—Anne!"

"You—you mean"—her voice dropped to a horrified whisper—*"murder?"*

Henry Walton leaned negligently back in his chair.

"If necessary," he said evenly. "But it should not be necessary. There are several ports of call between here and Talimi where he can be inadvertently left behind, and where he would have to remain out of communication with the rest of the world until the *Alola* touched there again a month later. But"—his voice sharpened suddenly— "from your rather logical deduction, I think you are really beginning to appreciate why I have been so frank with you, and to realize that we will permit nothing, not even consideration for a *daughter,* to interfere with—"

"Permit!" Her hands were clenching and unclenching at her sides, her head was thrown back, her eyes flashing. "You cannot stop me! Nothing can prevent me from interfering! Yes, I understand! You mean that so paltry a thing as my life would not be allowed to stand in the way. Oh, you have made it clear enough! But I shall stop it!"

"Indeed!" murmured Henry Walton. "And how, my dear Anne?"

"By going down to Suva now—by shouting it out aloud through the town if necessary," she answered passionately.

"Very effective—but a bit hysterical, don't you think?" drawled Henry Walton. "And so you would deliver your own flesh and blood, your father, over to the police?"

"Yes!" she declared. "Under the circumstances, yes—a thousand times yes!"

Henry Walton's eyes fixed in a strange, brooding glow upon Anne's face.

"Once caught," he said in a curious musing voice, "I would, on account of this and on account of certain episodes in the past, either swing from the gallows or spend the rest of my life in prison."

"Then stop this thing now!" Anne cried.

Henry Walton shook his head.

"It is an *impasse* so far," he said coldly. "You, of course, will never be allowed to open your lips anyway; but, if your relationship to me is a factor that you are determined to ignore, have you thought of what disclosure will mean to yourself? Rather a ruined life, I should say, my dear! Where would you go to live the shame of it down?"

"Yes; I have thought of that!" Anne answered instantly. "But you have already robbed me of what I care for most."

"Still an *impasse,*" said Henry Walton—and leaned suddenly toward her across the table. "You spoke a moment ago about 'so paltry a thing as your life.' As you know, I am not alone in this. Nothing could save you if, in the jargon, you peached. You would not weigh down the balance against a hundred thousand pounds."

"I am not afraid of your threats," Anne replied, and there was a quietness in her voice that surprised herself. "I would far rather die than buy my life like a miserable coward at the price of being a criminal too."

Henry Walton nodded his head.

"Yes; quite so!" he said judicially. "Knowing you as I do, Anne, I believe you literally. I did not expect anything else. But you mentioned price. Let us speak of that as a last resort—since I seemed to have failed in all other directions."

The blood flamed angry red in Anne's cheeks. "Oh," she burst out wildly, "I loathe you for that! You dare to suggest that I can be bribed by, I suppose, a share of what you expect your vile thuggery to bring you—that—that I have my price!"

"As every one else in the world has," observed Henry Walton with a tolerant smile. "Even those quite as honest and with the same upstanding integrity as yourself, my dear. But the price is not necessarily one of money or riches or worldly wealth, though the great majority fall into that category; with some it is the desire for fame and notoriety; with some it is the desire for revenge, the satisfying of the cravings of hate; with some it is the desire for power—but, whether the baser or the higher motives are the impelling force, the man or woman has yet to be born who, in some form or other, has not his or her price. With you, my dear Anne, it is —love."

"Love!" She felt the blood recede from her cheeks. "What—what do you mean?" she stammered.

"Exactly what I say," he answered. "You have already experienced that psychological moment to which I referred on that afternoon before the storm. And, from your slightly delirious state during the following few days, I gathered that you experienced it in the storm itself. You love Donald Lane."

"And if I do!" she said in a low voice. "I am a criminal's daughter—a daughter of a felon. I have nothing now to hope for any more from my love."

"Perhaps not," he said coolly; "but that in no way affects the fact that *your* love for him still remains."

Anne drew her hands across her eyes. Her mind, her brain, were tired and weary and in distress.

"I—I do not understand," she said.

He stood up abruptly, and, leaning against the table, stared at her for a moment in silence.

Mechanically Anne drew back a pace. His face seemed to have undergone a sudden transformation. It was grim and sinister in every feature. The thought came to her that she was gazing, not at a face, but at a naked soul. It was as though a mask had been withdrawn. The habitually pleasant expression of the polished gentleman which had earned for Mr. Henry Walton so many friends had disappeared as though it had never existed. There was evil in his eyes; and, added to the cruelty in the set lips, an ugly finality in their droop at the corners of his mouth. His voice alone was unchanged—it retained its horrible note of casualness.

"I do not wish to indulge in heroics, Anne," he said. "We will admit, if you wish, that I am an inhuman parent—but I can claim no originality on that score. From the beginning of time fathers, mothers, son, daughters, wives and husbands have dabbled their hands in each others' blood unrestrained by their ties of kindred. I entertain a certain repugnance toward that kind of thing, but I do not balk at it if it is the only means of removing an obstacle that stands in my way. I allow no one to stand in my way—and you shall not do so. This thing is going through to the end. It cannot go through if you *talk*. You are attractive and at times you have been useful to me, but I cannot say that I have ever had any exaggerated affection for you; if you refuse to keep silent your lips must be sealed for you—and sealed they will be. I have already said I believed your statement that you would not buy even your life that way. I believe that utterly—because I know you perhaps better than you do yourself. But what you will not buy for the sake of your own life, I think you will buy for another's. If it becomes necessary to put *you* out of the way, it makes very little difference if still another is added to the list. I refer to Donald Lane—in a sense an innocent by-stander."

Horror was in Anne's face; an overwhelming and sudden terror was in her heart. She clutched at her throat.

"You—you mean," she faltered, "that—that unless I promise you will—will kill Donald, too?"

"Yes," he said calmly. "It is a disagreeable word, isn't it? Are you wondering how it could be accomplished? Very simply. This is a lonely place. A message from you sent to Donald Lane would bring him here hot-foot. And what hour of the twenty-four could be better than the present one? You would both disappear. I fancy it would be called an elopement—due to the trouble that is known to exist between his uncle and your father."

"You—you are a fiend!" she cried out. "A monstrous, inhuman fiend!"

"As you will!" said Henry Walton, with another shrug of his shoulders. "I am resorting to the only method I have of saving your life—by forcing you to save it or else sacrifice another's. You see, I much prefer the pleasanter and the easier way— your word that you will say nothing to any one of anything you have heard to-night. Simply that."

"My word?" she repeated mechanically. "Just my word? You would take that?"

"Because I know that, once given, you would never break it," he said.

She turned, groping once more for the chair, and, dropping into it, buried her face again in her hands. She did not doubt him—did not doubt his threats. He was too horrible to doubt. She had read his ghastly sincerity in his eyes, in his face— because she had seen his soul there. Doubt him? There was no room for doubt. If only there were! But she was only too sure, too certain. She had seen him at his butchery with her own eyes. Franchon! She shuddered—and cried out. And the girl Tisotte! Madame Frigon had seen that—the thrust of a knife without provocation, and as coolly done as though "he was lighting a cigarette!" There was no question of doubt. Her mind tried to grapple with the problem. If it were merely her own life, then—no! She would have been a coward then. But Donald's! Donald's life for a few jewels! She wanted to scream out, laugh hysterically at such a hideous notion. She fought for self-control. It wasn't much, not very much to to—to keep criminally silent for—for Donald's life. She couldn't prevent the crime, she couldn't tell anybody about it anyway—they would never let her leave this room. Tell anybody! Perhaps she *could* prevent it—another way—without risk to anybody but herself—and—and still keep her word.

"I am waiting for an answer," Henry Walton prompted sharply. "And there is some one else who is also waiting—in my room."

Anne looked up. Her face was bloodless, haggard.

"I will give my word," she said slowly, "that I will never repeat anything of what I have heard tonight, and that I will never denounce you for what you are, or say anything that will ever put anybody upon your track; but I will not make of myself any more of an accomplice than that, and—and if there is anything I can do by myself alone to stop you, I will do it."

"Any such efforts on your part, my dear," said Mr. Walton with a grim smile, "will, I am sure, inject a very desirable touch of amusement into an otherwise somewhat drab affair. I invite you most heartily to try. For the rest, I congratulate you on your decision. I will leave the lamp with you, Anne. Good-night, my dear."

Anne did not answer, did not move from her chair—and when, hours later, daylight came, she was still there, staring with unseeing eyes about her, unconscious that the lamp was still burning upon the table.

CHAPTER VI   THE MYSTERIOUS PASSENGER

THE *Alola* had sailed at five o'clock that afternoon. It was nearly dinner time now. Anne stared at herself in the mirror over her cabin washstand. She looked tired and ill; but it struck her as something strangely like a miracle that the face which gazed back at her possessed any resemblance at all to her own. She was not the same Anne as yesterday; the yesterdays had passed away forever, and with them had passed her old self. It was strange that a new entity should not have brought with it a complete and corresponding change of features!

She coiled the long, glossy braids of rich brown hair with fingers that, usually so deft, hesitated a little now. She had come aboard long before sailing time—she had insisted on that. She could not have faced the good-byes to everybody in the town. And since coming on board she had deliberately kept to her stateroom—but it had merely postponed the inevitable meeting with Donald Lane. She wanted to see him, with all her soul she wanted to be near him, to look at him; but she dreaded the meeting. It would be the final act of renouncing the greatest happiness she had ever known. And she dreaded the meeting on still another score. He would never understand—and since she could never now by either word or look offer him an explanation, or even hint at one, since that was the very essence of the bargain she had made to save his life, she must let him go out of her life that way. Would he make the pain still harder to endure with his contempt for a woman who played fast and loose with a man's love—because he did not understand?

Under ordinary circumstances the plea of illness could have kept her in her cabin until Talimi was reached; it would have been better for him and better for her; it would have saved them both a great deal—but there was something else now, something that prohibited her from doing that, something that took precedence, since anything there had ever been between Donald Lane and herself could be no more than a memory hereafter.

There was something else now. Her mind kept constantly reverting to Donald, but—but she must try not to think of him—it tortured her so. There was something else. She had fought it all out with herself that morning in the hours before the dawn. She had made her decision. Her father would never rob John Crane if she could help it! It did not matter what the personal result to herself might be—that was of no moment. She would risk anything that involved herself alone, dare anything while still keeping strictly to her promise, to prevent the theft from being carried out.

She shivered suddenly. That it should be John Crane, which was almost the same as though it were Donald himself, made the misery and the shame of it all the more starkly abhorrent. She *would* stop it! She did not know how—but somehow—in spite of an almost panic-fear that she was attempting the impossible. That was the only reason she had come aboard the *Alola,* and was going for the last time to Talimi. Her father did not realize that; he had taken it as a matter of course that she should go back with him to the island. She had scarcely spoken a word to him since last night. Afterwards—but what did the "afterwards" or the future matter in the sense that they demanded any concrete plans? The future was a blank except that somewhere, where she was not known, she would live out the rest of her life—somehow. Further association with her father and his wretched, evil life was not only detestable, but impossible; Talimi, supported by the proceeds of crime so vile that even yet she could not grasp the awfulness of it in its entirety, was no longer a home.

But if she had come aboard the *Alola* for a purpose, she certainly could not accomplish it by remaining here shut up in her cabin—to avoid Donald Lane. Well, she had no intention of doing so. It was only an hour since they had sailed, and she had granted herself that hour as a little respite, the final one, before facing the ordeal that was to come.

Yet, even so, she had not been altogether idle. From her cabin port-hole, before the *Alola* sailed, she had been able, unobserved herself, to watch everybody on the wharf, and particularly those who came up the gangway. Her first task, she knew, was to establish the identity of the immediate victim of her father's rascality—the Russian ex-nobleman who carried the coveted credentials, and who, for very obvious reasons, was almost certain to be travelling in any other guise than that of a man going to Talimi with the frank and avowed purpose of redeeming all that was left to himself and his compatriots of wealth and possessions. Then there was equally the identity of her father's accomplice to establish—the man who had come to the bungalow last night.

Anne shook her head now dubiously. She had not been in any

way rewarded—but then so many people had come and gone across the gangway that it was impossible to tell who, out of them all, were even the ten or twelve passengers that, at most, would comprise the *Alola's* list. Still she had watched. There was *one* she would know.

She caught her breath slightly. Donald again! Yes, Donald again! She had watched eagerly, yet hoping more and more as he did not appear that he had cancelled his passage. She had sent him a note that morning, a studied and coldly formal note that left no doubt as to its finality, stating that she had made other arrangements for getting down to the *Alola,* and that it was not only quite unnecessary, but her choice that he should not come for her.

Her hair fell in a mass about her shoulders from fingers that had suddenly relaxed. It would hurt him, sting him with its cool indifference, its airy disposal of anything he might have been pleased to make out of the former note she had sent him by the doctor. And she had deliberately tried to make it so, because—because—oh, because it was the kindest thing she could do—to try to make him think of her in that way—the last woman in the world that Donald Lane would marry, would care to marry, was a flippant woman.

He had not cancelled his passage. At almost the last moment, she had seen his broad-shouldered figure come up the gangway. She had had only a glimpse of him; but the bandages were *not* all gone from his head—there was one just below the brim of his pith helmet—and his face had lost a great deal of its bronze, and he was thinner, and still looked ill, and—

From outside in the alleyway there came suddenly a deafening unmusical clamour like a frantic pounding upon a tin pan. It was the *Alola's* dinner gong. And almost coincidentally a knock sounded on her door.

"Are you coming to dinner, Anne, or shall I have something sent along to you?" It was her father's voice, cool, sauve, composed as ever.

"I will join you presently," she replied quietly.

"Right, you are!" he answered—and she heard his step passing on along the alleyway.

She completed her toilet hurriedly, and a few minutes later entered the ship's little saloon. It was a shabby place, as shabby and old-fashioned and out-of-date as the antiquated vessel itself. A long table ran down the centre, with a row of straight-backed, swivel chairs on either side. A glance told her that they were nearly all occupied. She had not been much out in her guess; there were some ten or eleven passengers—all men. Captain Croon's round, red face and bald head loomed up from the head of the table—and his voice bellowed jovially to her:

"Here you are, Miss Anne! Right here in the same seat you've had since you were a kiddie!"

Donald Lane was looking at her. She was conscious of that, conscious that he was seated at almost the extreme lower end of the table, though she did not dare to look at him. She—she was suddenly afraid of herself. She wanted to cry out piteously, helplessly. She steeled herself to bow composedly as she passed on to her seat.

She sat down and forced a smiling reply to the captain's greeting.

A moment later her father introduced her to her vis-a-vis, a dark-skinned, middle-aged man on the captain's left.

"A fellow passenger of mine on the *Makura* from Vancouver, my dear, whose company I am sure you would have enjoyed had you been with us," said Henry Walton pleasantly. "Monsieur Faradeau—my daughter, Anne. My daughter, as I may have mentioned to you on the voyage, came out a ship ahead of me in order to make a short visit to some friends in Auckland."

Monsieur Faradeau bowed profoundly.

"I am delighted and honoured to make mademoiselle's acquaintance," he said.

Anne murmured a formal acknowledgment. Her emotions had abruptly assumed a new and totally different phase. Behind the amber-coloured lenses of Henry Walton's pince-nez she thought she had caught a faint gleam of mockery. She was aware of a sudden, startled sense of excitement sweeping upon her. Monsieur Faradeau spoke with a slight trace of foreign accent that she did not think was *French*—like the name. He had come out on the *Makura* with her father; and his manners were decidedly those of a polished gentleman. The name was not Russian—but a Russian name was the last one she would expect an ex-nobleman of Russia to possess under the present circumstances.

"I was just saying," said Henry Walton genially, "that it was both a surprise and a pleasure to find Monsieur Faradeau aboard here. Of course, being up in the hills, I did not see him after we reached Suva; but I had understood him to say he was going on to Sydney, and from

94

there home by the P. and O."

Anne's eyes drifted to the man opposite her. Intuitively, she was *certain* of him now. His eyes had abruptly sought his plate, and, for all his ease of manner, his composure appeared to be suddenly somewhat disturbed.

"That is quite true, Monsieur Walton," the other said with almost exaggerated earnestness. "But, after all, I travel only for pleasure. Fiji enchanted me, and I was told that Captain Croon on his trip visited many islands that were even more beautiful."

"Which accounts for you being here on the *Alola,* of course!" observed Henry Walton softly.

Anne glanced quickly at her father—in time to catch an enigmatical little smile playing around the corners of his mouth.

"Yes, monsieur—precisely," replied Monsieur Faradeau.

"Well, you'll find them more primitive anyway," said Henry Walton heartily; "and in that way, at least, more interesting—to the sight-seer. I don't blame you at all."

Anne's eyes roved now up and down the table, as she chatted with the captain. To her relief Donald Lane was on the same side as herself and she could not see him.

"I see you have the usual passenger list, Captain Croon," she said.

"Just about!" the captain answered. "Planters going back home; and agents going out to get an option on copra and that sort of stuff from owners like your father—and commercial men looking after their fences. Yes, just about, Miss Anne— just about!"

"You overlook Monsieur Faradeau," broke in Henry Walton laughingly. "And if he is an exception, he is at least a distinguished one. You're no swanky mail boat, Croon, and it's not often you have a tourist out for pleasure."

Her father was deliberately baiting the man. Anne caught a startled look, come and gone in an instant, in Monsieur Faradeau's eyes. But her father was baiting *her* too! He was deliberately telling her that *this* was the man. It was just like her father; he would enjoy that sort of thing—to let her tug at the end of her chain from which, he was quite certain, she could not break loose!

The round-faced skipper smiled good-naturedly.

"Well, I'm not saying I am," he said; "but Monsieur Faradeau might do a lot worse. If he wants to see islands that are the real genuine article and warranted to put the beauty of Eden in the second class, he couldn't do better than he's doing."

"I am sure that is true, captain," Monsieur Faradeau spoke quickly—and, it seemed to Anne, a little over-eagerly, as though anxious to vindicate himself. "From what I have already seen, I love the islands—they intoxicate me."

"My word!" said Mr. Henry Walton—and again Anne caught the enigmatical smile playing around the corners of his mouth. "There's genuine enthusiasm for you! But, I say, Croon, if I were you, I'd look out for myself! Unless he's paid the round passage in advance I wouldn't risk letting him ashore anywhere. The lure of one of these super-Eden spots of yours might be too much for him— and he'd give you the slip."

"And quite right he'd be, too!" Captain Croon nodded heartily at Monsieur Faradeau. "You'd have something to talk about when you got home, and I'd pick you up on the way back."

"Good Lord!" exclaimed Henry Walton. "I'm not serious!"

Anne was toying now with the food on her plate. There were two men at the table here that she was trying to identify; no—*one.* One, she was already satisfied, there could be no doubt about. Monsieur Faradeau! Her father was amusing himself with the man—doing more than that—very craftily throwing dust in the captain's eyes. Monsieur Faradeau would, if her father had his way, undoubtedly succumb to the lure of one of the islands between here and Talimi; and the *Alola,* quite unsuspicious that anything was wrong, would sail on minus a passenger.

But the other man! Her father's accomplice— the man who had been at the bungalow last night! Quite unostentatiously, while she joined at intervals in the conversation around her, she studied her fellow passengers at the table—and acknowledged herself hopelessly at a loss. And it frightened her a little. All her life she had lived in the islands, and she knew the types of the tropics very thoroughly. They were distinctive. Every one of these men here was true to type. That one of them could have come but recently from Paris and still play his part so well, predicated a degree of cleverness that brought a surge of dismay upon her at the thought of attempting to cope with this ugly plot that knew its head and brains in this man beside her—her father.

She grew silent. She could not shake off a sense of growing depression. She heard Captain Croon say something about making

Matalofa a little after daybreak. She heard her father laugh.

"The cream of them all!" cried Henry Walton. "'The coral-girdled, palm-crowned gem of Polynesia, as the poets would say! Matalofa's the place for you, Faradeau! Wait till you see it!"

The meal ended.

Anne rose from her seat; and Captain Croon, appropriating her arm, laughingly tucked it under his own.

"The only chance we old fellows have got—eh, what—Miss Anne? I'm going on the bridge by and by, but until then the young chaps have got to sheer off while we have a turn on deck."

"Yes," she said inaudibly—she was passing by Donald Lane again.

They made their way up to the combination promenade and boat deck, and began to pace around it. Captain Croon alternately related all the latest gossip of the islands and plied her with questions about herself.

She listened mechanically, and answered mechanically. She wanted to get away somewhere to think —she must *think*. Even Donald did not intrude upon her thoughts now. Her father's words about Matalofa kept reiterating themselves in her mind. They would touch Matalofa a little after daybreak. There wasn't much time. Matalofa was the first port of call, then one or two smaller islands during the day, and, in the evening, Talimi. She knew which one of the passengers was the Russian now, and she was convinced it was at Matalofa that he was to be marooned—if not worse than marooned.

Her father, she was quite sure, had not only said what he had for the purpose of preparing Captain Croon for Monsieur Faradeau's enforced decision to remain at Matalofa, but he had taken a malicious delight in doing so in her, Anne's, presence as a—a sort of contemptuous gibe at her helplessness. But he would not have said what he had unless he were genuinely and supremely confident that nothing could interfere with his plans. She sensed that; felt that—and it brought renewed dismay. He was clever, callous, ruthless—with another, quite as unscrupulous as himself, at his back. She was alone— a girl. What was she to do?

Around and around the deck she walked, walked interminably, the skipper's voice droning in her ears, her laughter rippling out at times because he laughed—she did not know at what; while over and over again one question hammered frantically at her brain and clamoured desperately for an answer, for the time was growing miserably short— just from now until daybreak.

What was she to do?

CHAPTER VII   A SECRET CONFERENCE

DONALD LANE was not in a good humour. He had followed Anne from the saloon, and, standing now unobtrusively in the shadow of one of the deck houses, he mentally cursed Captain Croon with fervency and abandon. Up and down, up and down! Did the man imagine, just because he commanded the benighted old scow, that he could appropriate Anne forever!

He wanted to talk to Anne—and he meant to do so, in spite of the fact that she had very noticeably and obviously avoided him. He had thought his chance would have come up here on deck immediately after she had left the saloon, but Captain Croon clung on and on.

What was the matter with Anne? What had happened? He stood pulling viciously at his cigarette—his eyes lighting up as his gaze followed her while she was in sight on his side of the deck; a frown, puzzled and heavy, furrowing his forehead as she turned the corner of the captain's cabin beneath the bridge and was lost to his view again. Her note of the night before! It couldn't have had any meaning but one—just one. It had made him a king among men, a superman—it had brought him the love of the woman that meant more to him, would always mean more to him than all else besides, the love, tender and true and staunch, that would last while life endured. Tender and true and staunch! Yes, she was! He wouldn't believe anything else. It was impossible! Not Anne! Any other woman perhaps—but not Anne, with those great brown eyes that looked at one so steadily and frankly, and in their smile held a treasure trove of loyalty and trust and faith, and somewhere latent in their depths the promise of a love-light that would shine out like a thing of glory for him who kindled it.

He had not seen that light there yet in her eyes. But he was sure, sure that it was there for him to see—sure that it was he who would kindle it.

Sure? He had been sure last night. But to-day? That other note—her avoidance of him! What did it mean? Could it have been her father—that long-seated trouble between her father and his uncle? Had she been mistaken in her father's attitude? Her father might have been complacent enough up to a certain point—until he became aware that it was a question of far more than mere friendship between his daughter and John Crane's nephew. And Mr. Walton must have become aware of that. If the doctor, with a sly twinkle in his eye, had dropped hints to him, Donald Lane, of things Anne had said when, in those first few days, she had been a little delirious, then certainly Mr. Walton would have heard, not only quite as much as the doctor, but a good deal more. Was it that?

He shook his head a little helplessly. He did not know. It was what he wanted to know. He wanted to know what had happened to change her like this. He was not angry; he was not hurt— he was desperately worried, desperately anxious. Angry! Hurt! With Anne! How could he be —even if he did not love her? They had told him what she had done in that storm, what she had risked to save his life.

She was passing by along the deck again. He watched her hungrily, the slim grace of her, the curve of the white neck, the poise of the dainty head. It was growing dark—twilight in the tropics was almost a momentary thing, just a splash of crimson sky in the west that was fading away now. He could not see her face. His hands tightened. Intense yearning surged upon him. He wanted her —to hold her, to fold his arms around her, to pillow her head upon his shoulder, to bury his face in her hair. What did it matter what had happened? Nothing should come between them! He would sweep it aside by brute force if necessary, trample it under foot—hurl it out of existence!

Perhaps *this* time Captain Croon would part company with her at the foot of the ladder there and go on the bridge! No; they had turned the corner again for still another round of the deck, or a dozen more, or—

A voice spoke suddenly and quietly at his elbow: "You are Monsieur Donald Lane, are you not?" He recognized the man as the one who had sat opposite Anne in the saloon.

"Yes," he answered; "that is my name."

"And mine, monsieur," said the other, "is Faradeau—Jules Faradeau."

Lane bowed perfunctorily. He was not in the slightest degree interested. Anne should be about halfway along the other side of the deck again.

"Monsieur Lane," said Monsieur Faradeau earnestly, "I beg you to forgive me, a stranger, for intruding myself upon you; but there is something I want to say that is of the utmost importance."

"All right," said Lane; "go ahead—though I don't see how there could be anything of a very important nature between us."

Monsieur Faradeau lowered his voice.

"Not here," he said. "It is too dangerous. We must not be seen together. If monsieur will go to his cabin, I will join him there in a minute."

Lane stared—and then he frowned. It was a very strange request, a most peculiar one; but he was not so much concerned with that phase of it as he was with the fact that, if he complied, he would have to leave the deck—and Anne.

"Look here," he said bluntly, "what's the big idea?"

"Monsieur," said the other hurriedly, "I beg of you that we do not stand here together. You are the nephew of Monsieur John Crane of Talimi. It is a matter that affects your uncle—a very grave matter—perhaps one of life and death. Will you not do as I ask, monsieur?"

Donald Lane leaned tensely forward. His uncle —a matter of perhaps life and death! There was no mistaking the anxiety in the other's voice, or the trouble and distress in the man's face.

"Yes, I will—if it's as bad as that!" he said tersely. "I'll see you in my cabin at once. Do you know where it is?"

"Yes," Monsieur Faradeau answered. "I know where it is."

"All right!" Lane nodded—and,—turning abruptly, walked quickly to the companionway and made his way down below.

He had barely turned on the light in his cabin and seated himself on the edge of his bunk—leaving the settee opposite for his self-invited guest— when Monsieur Faradeau, after knocking softly, entered and closed the door noiselessly behind him.

Lane motioned toward the settee.

Monsieur Faradeau sat down.

"Now," said Lane briskly, "what is it?"

"Monsieur Lane," said Monsieur Faradeau in a guarded voice, "did your uncle ever say anything to you about a package that was left in trust with him—a package of very great value?"

Donald Lane's face hardened suddenly. His uncle most certainly *had* spoken to him about such a package, and, not only spoken about it, but had shown him where it was kept. John Crane was a methodical man. "In case anything happens to me," John Crane had said, "you'll know what it is, and where it is." Lane stared hard now at Monsieur Faradeau.

"From a complete stranger, that's rather a leading question, isn't it?" he inquired evenly.

Monsieur Faradeau nodded his head quickly.

"Yes," he said earnestly; "it is. I began awkwardly. See, then, monsieur—look here! Let me prove my good faith". He fumbled for a moment inside his shirt bosom, and drew out a sealed envelope; this he tore open, and extracted from within a folded slip of paper which he handed to Donald Lane.

"Good God!" exclaimed Lane sharply, as he glanced at the paper. "This is the list, written by my uncle, of what that package contains!"

"You know the story?" said Monsieur haradeau quietly.

"Yes; in a general way," Lane answered. "My uncle told me the gist of it—not with any idea of betraying a confidence, but as a safeguard and a precaution should anything happen to him, in which case this"—he tapped the slip of paper with his finger—"or, rather, what it represents, would otherwise be lost to its owners."

"I judged as much," said Monsieur Faradeau gravely. "Are you quite satisfied, then, Monsieur Lane, with my good faith, and that the paper there is in your uncle's handwriting?"

"There is no question about it, Monsieur Faradeau," Lane responded promptly.

Monsieur Faradeau passed his hand nervously across his eyes.

"My name is not Faradeau"—he smiled a little wearily—"it is the second one on the list. But Faradeau, I think, monsieur, will serve us best."

Lane glanced at the list again. The second name was Count Alexis Mirakoff; and opposite the name was entered: "The chamois bag of unset stones."

"Yes," he said; "I understand—we'll stick to 'Faradeau.' But why have you come to me? You are obviously on your way out to my uncle to redeem the package, and to-morrow night you will be at Talimi."

"I have come to you," the other replied, "because you are the only man, since you are Monsieur Crane's nephew, that I can trust; and I have come to you because I am afraid."

"Afraid?" Lane echoed the word tensely.

Monsieur Faradeau shook his head slowly.

"Not for myself," he said, and the weary smile crept around his lips again; "but for that paper in your hand. I am only *one* of those whose names are written there."

"You mean," said Lane quickly, "that you have reason to believe you have been followed by Soviet agents, and that you are in danger here aboard this ship?"

Monsieur Faradeau remained thoughtful for a moment before he answered.

"It *was* the Soviet agents," he said at last; "I am not sure whether it still is nor not. I knew that one of them had overtaken me in New York— there might have been more than one—but that one I recognized. He was killed— murdered. I do not know by whom. It would imply that other agencies were at work, and I believe I *am* still being followed. I am not sure, I do not know; I have doubled and redoubled on my tracks—but I am afraid. They would not openly show their hands anyway until they had discovered my destination, for otherwise my death or that paper would be valueless to them. Whether that is yet known to them or not, I do not know. But now, at almost the last moment—you may call it intuition if you like—I am very much afraid. I dare not take any chance that can possibly be avoided. That is why I have come to you."

"But nothing has happened so far on board here, has there?" questioned Lane in a serious voice. "Nothing to lead you to suspect any one in particular?"

"Nothing." There was a tired and overwrought note in Monsieur Faradeau's voice. "But I suspect *everybody*—except one man, who, because he is virtually John Crane, cannot be suspected. That is yourself, Monsieur Lane."

"Naturally!" Lane smiled. "That's logical enough. But what do you want me to do?"

"I want you to keep that paper for me," said Monsieur Faradeau soberly. "If anything happens to me, the package will still be safe, and your uncle can communicate with Monsieur Todd. If everything goes well, you can return it to me at Talimi. I do not ask this for my own sake, Monsieur Lane; I ask it for the sake of others. Will you do it?"

Donald Lane took out his pocketbook, opened it, placed the slip of paper inside, and returned the leather case to his pocket.

"Certainly, I will," he said heartily.

Monsieur Faradeau stood up and wrung Donald Lane's hand fervently.

"I have no words to thank you," he said huskily. "I shall sleep easier to-night than I have for many weeks." He motioned toward the door. "If the way is clear, I will go. Will you look, monsieur? We must not take any risk of it being known we were here together."

Donald Lane opened the door and looked out. The narrow little alleyway was empty.

"It's all right," he said.

Again Monsieur Faradeau wrung Donald Lane's hand.

"I am very grateful, monsieur!" he whispered— and slipped silently out into the alleyway.

Lane lighted a cigarette and puffed at it thoughtfully for a few minutes.

"A bit of a rum go, as they say out here!" he muttered finally to himself. "Uncle's got the package, and I've got the 'open sesame' to it! Upon my soul, I hope nothing happens to that chap!"

His thoughts reverted to Anne. Captain Croon would certainly have left her by now. He switched off his light and went on deck. There was no sign of Anne. Captain Croon, he could see as he went forward, was on the bridge. It was dark, of course; she might have drawn a chair into some secluded nook. He made a circuit of the deck; and thereafter of the ship from end to end. There was still no sign of Anne. She must be in her cabin. He went down below again, and called one of the native stewards.

"Go to Miss Walton's cabin," he instructed, "and say that Mr. Lane would very much like to see her for a few minutes."

The boy returned with the information that there had been no response from the cabin.

Donald Lane went up on deck again, and this time entered the smoking-room. Mr. Walton was playing bridge with three of his fellow passengers. At the moment he was dummy.

"Do you know where Miss Walton is, sir?" Lane asked.

Mr. Walton looked up with a cordial smile.

"I'm sure I don't," he said. "She was out on deck a little while ago. She must be somewhere about."

Lane left the smoking-room, and, crossing to the ship's rail, stood staring out at a sea that, quiet save for its smooth, rolling swells, had the sheen of satin in it under the moonlight. She wasn't on deck. She wasn't "somewhere about."

"Damn!" said Donald Lane—and he said it from his soul.

CHAPTER VIII   A LONE HAND

FOUR bells—two o'clock in the morning.

Anne cautiously opened the door of her cabin, and looked out into the alleyway. She was still fully dressed. She had not been in bed, save in the sense that face down on her bunk she had wrestled in the darkness with her problem from the moment almost that she had finally and in desperation made an excuse to get away from Captain Croon. She had heard the steward knock upon her door hours before; she had heard once or twice a footstep in the alleyway that she had recognized as Donald Lane's, and, after midnight, had heard his door, which she knew to be the second one beyond her father's, open and close. After that, for an hour, there had been other footsteps now and then, the opening and closing of other doors; but now it was still and quiet—except only for the groan and creak and wheeze of the ship itself, complaining bitterly in every one of its aged joints as it rolled and pitched in almost a calm sea.

She caught her breath a little, as she stepped out now into the alleyway. The hours had brought her a solution, though the consequences to herself were—

Her lips drew together; her hand that, hidden in the folds of a small scarf gripped her revolver, clutched the weapon a little more tenaciously. She had started out with the premise that the consequences to herself were to be ignored, but the consequences loomed very large now that she was about to put her plan into execution. Suppose—suppose that— *No!* She would not suppose at all! She would not at the last moment let herself be frightened into retreat. There was only one way; or, at least, she had been able to devise only one way— and that was to persuade Monsieur Faradeau to get rid of the paper he carried before Matalofa was reached, which would be in a few hours now. She could not explain to Monsieur Faradeau—her pledge forbade that; but from the very nature of that paper the man must be conscious he was never free from danger, and she counted upon that fact, and upon what would surely be obvious to him— her sincerity—to accomplish her purpose. It was a very simple suggestion that she proposed to make —one that could in no possible way arouse suspicion of double-dealing in his mind. It was merely that he should go now, at once, to Captain Croon's cabin, wake the captain, and have the paper locked in the ship's safe until they got to

Talimi. Without that paper Monsieur Faradeau became of no more interest to her father; without that paper her father could do nothing. But to accomplish her whole purpose, to make her plan effective in saving Monsieur Faradeau himself from attack, her father must know what she had done—and therein lay the consequences to herself—and she must *invite* them. Once the paper was safe, she had no choice but to go at once to her father's room and defy him openly.

It seemed as though she could hear the beating of her heart as she went swiftly forward along the alleyway. She *was* a little afraid, but she would go on, she must go on. Her revolver—the weapon hidden in her scarf? She was going to do a very daring thing for a woman— this visit to Monsieur Faradeau's room—at this hour. She did not know what kind of a man in *character* Monsieur Faradeau might prove to be. But it was not for that reason alone she carried the weapon; it was for the afterwards where no uncertainty existed as to whether she would require protection or not—when she went to her father.

Monsieur Faradeau's cabin was on the other side of the ship, and near the cross-alleyway in front of the saloon—she had seen the man go into his room when she had come down the companionway after leaving Captain Croon. Anne reached the cross-alleyway, where a light was burning—and halted abruptly, a little startled. And then she laughed to herself nervously. It was only the movement of the ship and the reflection from the polished surface of the huge metal gong which stood on a sort of built-in buffet that faced the entrance to the saloon; it had seemed as though some one had suddenly flung a ray of light full upon her.

Anne listened now as she looked about her. At both ends of the cross-alleyway a door opened on the narrow lower deck, which in turn gave on the after part of the ship where access could again be had to the cabins. She smiled a little wanly to herself. There was no reason why she should notice these doors, was there?—as though she were a thief taking note of possible avenues of escape! Why not the companionways then, also on either hand, that led to the boat deck above? How the ship creaked and made eerie noises! The engines thumped, thumped, thumped like dull blows being struck somewhere; and voices, the voices of ancient bulkheads and stanchions answered, moaning as though in pain. Her heart began to thump in tempo with the engines. The colour had ebbed slightly from her face.

"You are afraid already—before there is anything to be afraid of!" Anne whispered bitterly— and crossed to the other alleyway and halted before a door.

She knocked softly. There was no answer. She knocked again, a little louder, more insistently— and this time with success.

"Who is there?" a voice demanded.

"Open the door, Monsieur Faradeau," Anne said quickly. "I must speak to you, and—and, please hurry!"

She heard a smothered exclamation and then the rattle of the key in the lock, and the door opened. She stepped hastily inside and closed the door behind her.

"Mon Dieu!" gasped Monsieur Faradeau. "There was very little light out there, but it is you, Mademoiselle Walton, is it not?"

"Yes," said Anne. She fought for control of her voice. "It—it is a little unconventional, isn't it? I—"

"But—but I do not understand!" Monsieur Faradeau interrupted in an amazed and perplexed voice. "It—it is incomprehensible! Mademoiselle Walton comes to my room in the middle of the night!"

Anne could just barely make out the pyjama-clad figure that stood before her. In the darkness she felt her cheeks flush crimson.

"Because," she said steadily, "you and the paper you carry are in danger."

"Paper! Danger!" Monsieur Faradeau echoed the words in a helpless tone of voice. "This is very strange! I know of no paper, mademoiselle."

The reply for a moment staggered Anne—but only for a moment. Naturally, the last thing Monsieur Faradeau would do would be to admit the possession of that paper to anybody—unless he were convinced that his possession of it was so intimately known that denial was useless.

"The paper I refer to," said Anne quietly, "is one you are taking to Mr. John Crane at Talimi, and it is in connection with a package of Russian jewels that is worth a very great sum of money."

"Mademoiselle," said Monsieur Faradeau blankly, "are you mad? No; it is that you are perhaps not well! You are ill, Mademoiselle?" —anxiously.

"No," Anne answered; "I am neither mad nor ill. Why do you act like this? I cannot tell you how I came to know that you have the paper, or how I know about the package, nor may I tell you the source of your danger; but I have come here at great risk to warn you—surely you can appreciate that as a proof of my sincerity."

"Mademoiselle," said Monsieur Faradeau gravely, "I appreciate so well the consequences to yourself if you were seen coming to my cabin, or were known to have been here at this hour, that I beg of you for your own sake to go back at once to your room. I do not know anything about any paper or package."

Had she made a mistake? A cold feeling of disaster settled upon Anne. On what, after all, had she based her supposition that Monsieur Faradeau here was the man her father proposed to victimize? On nothing that was really tangible—nothing but a dinner-table conversation that was perhaps mere banter on her father's part, and upon which she had allowed her imagination to place a wholly different construction. If it was a mistake, it was a miserable one—it meant *disaster*. There was little or no time in which to retrieve it—little or no opportunity to start afresh on a search for the "right" man.

She leaned back against the bulkhead at the edge of the door, fighting for composure, struggling to make up her mind what to do. The man's manner, his voice, what he said, all seemed unquestionably convincing—and yet, somehow, she could not still believe that she was wrong.

"I wanted to get you to ask Captain Croon to put it in his safe," she burst out desperately. "Do you think I am trying to play some game to get the paper away from you? Can't you understand that I am only trying to save you—and it?"

"But mademoiselle" — Monsieur Faradeau's voice came patiently through the darkness—"I have already explained that I know nothing of what you are talking about. Mademoiselle, again I beg of you to think of yourself, and return to your room."

If she could only see his face! His voice was sincere and genuine enough—but it was not always so easy to disguise one's features. If she could only see his face suddenly—take him by surprise! It was merely snatching at a straw perhaps—but she was desperate enough to snatch at anything. The electric-light switch in her cabin was at the side of the door; it was probably in the same position here —just where she was standing. She felt out with her hand. Yes; here it was! There was a faint *click*—and the cabin was flooded with light.

Monsieur Faradeau blinked his eyes—and then shrugged his shoulders helplessly.

108

"Really, mademoiselle," he expostulated, "you place me in a—a very embarrassing position. A scene here would be—how shall I say it?—so very compromising for mademoiselle's good name, and I should regret so much to have to resort to force. Please go at once, mademoiselle!"

She was beaten. The expostulation, even the hint of contempt that had crept into his voice, was mirrored in his face and eyes. The colour came crimsoning her cheeks again. Besides the knowledge of defeat and disaster, there was a sense of shame that crowded itself upon her, humiliated her, tortured her. What did this man *think* of her!

She half turned to open the door—and stood suddenly motionless. For a moment she was dazed, incredulous, bewildered— then she faced Monsieur Faradeau again, a queer and ominous little smile upon her lips.

Hanging from a hook above the settee was the same checkered cap she had picked up from the floor of the bungalow the night before when she had knocked the table over!

Anne's hand, freed from the scarf, swung swiftly out from her side—and Monsieur Faradeau was staring into the muzzle of her revolver.

"You—you *almost* won, didn't you?" said Anne with a strange little catch in her voice.

"Won, mademoiselle?" Monsieur Faradeau's tones were those of blank amazement—but he hastily retreated a step. "I do not—"

"But *I* do—now!" said Anne coldly. "The role of Monsieur Faradeau may have been admirably played, but it is at an end. You are probably no more French than I am. I am certain, however, of two things about you: first, that you are a murderous scoundrel; and, second, that, instead of being the man I was trying to warn, you are the man I overheard plotting your fiendish scheme with my father in the bungalow last night."

"Mad—yes!" murmured Monsieur Faradeau helplessly. "That is it! She is mad!"

Anne pointed to the cap hanging above the settee.

"You perhaps do not remember that you had placed that cap on the table in the hall of the bungalow; but you will remember that I knocked the table over, since that is how my father discovered my presence there."

The man's face changed colour slightly.

The man's eyes went to the cap, roved from there around the room, fixed finally upon Anne—and into them came a cat-like gleam as he appeared to measure the distance between them.

Anne's lips curled grimly.

"Don't try it!" she advised. "If you move an inch toward me, I will fire without the slightest compunction."

"What do you want?" Monsieur Faradeau demanded hoarsely.

"I want to know where that paper is, and who the man is that has got it?"

Monsieur Faradeau glanced at her sullenly, but made no reply.

"I came here," said Anne, "expecting to find and, if I could, help a man who was being victimized; instead, I find a man who, tacitly at least, in common with my father, threatened my life last night. You will report this visit to my father, and afterwards, I suppose, unless I can save myself in some way, I will pay the penalty. But first I am going to put an end to this miserable business that is going on here. Is that quite clear? Do you expect me to hesitate now when it is merely a choice between putting a bullet into a creature such as you, or allowing an innocent man to be marooned and, in all probability, done away with? You may refuse to answer and force me to shoot, but it is absolutely certain that if anything happened to you it would just as effectively put a stop to this abominable affair. My father could not afford to appear in it personally—he would not dare present that paper in person to John Crane. Well?"

Monsieur Faradeau's eyes met Anne's, held for an instant, and dropped. His face had suddenly gone white.

"By God, I—I believe you would!" he muttered. "We ought to have finished you last night!"

"Who is the man, and where is the paper?" repeated Anne monotonously.

Monsieur Faradeau stood for a moment with twitching lips, and then suddenly he began to laugh a little raucously.

"Oh, all right—you she-cat!" he snarled. "Seeing it won't do you any good anyhow, and since your father seems to think it is quite safe to confide in you, there's no use my risking your shot for nothing. The man is your very dear friend Donald Lane, and the paper is in Donald Lane's pocket-book."

For the fraction of a second the revolver in Anne's hand wavered; and for the fraction of a second the cabin seemed to whirl around her.

"Donald Lane!" Her voice was low, shaken, unsteady. "How— how did he get it? Why has he got it?"

Monsieur Faradeau shrugged his shoulders.

That's a question you'd better ask your father," he sneered; "he —"

"I will!" Anne interrupted, a sudden thrill in her voice. I will— after I have got the paper!"

Monsieur Faradeau was obviously startled. His jaw sagged heavily.

"You— you *what!*" he gasped —and took a step toward her.

"Don't move!" Anne ordered sharply. "I've even more incentive to shoot you now than I had before!"

Monsieur Faradeau drew up with a jerk.

Anne backed to the door, and with her free hand removed the key from the lock; then, opening the door, she inserted the key on the other side. There was no more to be gained here. It was the paper now! At any cost she must have it. She couldn't go to Donald Lane as she had come to this man— but there was another way—a better way. A plan had come in a flash.

Her eyes were on Monsieur Faradeau. He was edging forward again. Anne smiled coldly—and on the instant fired at the floor. And then, with the roar of the shot still echoing through the ship, she sprang across the threshold, slammed the door with a loud crash, turned the key in the lock, and darted toward the cross-alleyway, firing again and again as she ran; then, swinging around the corner, she snatched at the great metal gong as she rushed past it, and sent it crashing to the floor with a deafening clatter.

The next instant she was out through the doorway on the same side of the ship as her own cabin, and was running along the lower deck toward the stern. From within she could hear a sudden sound of commotion—doors opening, voices raised in bewildered excitement. She gained the after entrance to the alleyway, and cautiously looked in. The occupants of the cabins were emerging from their various doorways, and were scurrying towards the forward end of the ship. She saw her father dashing hurriedly along in advance of everybody else; and she saw that Donald Lane's door was already open, and that he had left his light burning.

She entered the alleyway. No one paid any attention to her; she was coming from the *other* direction—simply one of the excited group that had been so rudely alarmed and aroused from sleep. Two men that she saw coming behind her, she allowed to pass—and then she slipped quickly into Donald Lane's cabin and closed the door.

She worked with frantic haste now. The pocket-book! It would probably be in his coat or vest. There were several suits hanging on the cabin wall. Swiftly she thrust her hand into, it seemed, a hundred pockets before she found the right one; and then with trembling fingers she began to search through the pocketbook itself. Suddenly she gave a little cry of triumph, thrust the pocketbook back into the pocket where she had found it, and rushed out of the cabin and into her own room three doors beyond.

The paper was in her possession.

CHAPTER IX MONSIEUR FARADEAU EXPLAINS

AS the shots and din had racketed through the ship Mr. Henry Walton had leaped from his bunk, and wrenched the door of his stateroom open. Other doors were being opened, pyjama-clad figures were emerging from the cabins, but Mr. Henry Walton, having perhaps a peculiar interest in any untoward event, and especially one of this nature that might transpire aboard the *Alola,* was by a small margin the first to reach the forward cross-alleyway from which direction the disturbance had seemed to come. He did not stop here, however. For perhaps very valid reasons he made at once for Monsieur Faradeau's room. The key on the outside of the door instantly caught his eye. It seemed to affect Mr. Henry Walton unhappily. He glanced sharply around him. Footsteps were pattering up the alleyways, voices were calling one to another, and the whole ship seemed to be seething with excitement—but no one as yet was near enough to observe him in the act of performing so minute a detail as that of turning a key in a lock. With a vicious oath under his breath, Mr. Henry Walton turned the key, at the same time extracting it from the lock, and swung the door open.

"You there, Weasel?" he demanded in a savage undertone. "What's all this about? Who locked you in? What the devil's the matter?"

Monsieur Faradeau, in anything but Monsieur Faradeau's polished voice, answered him.

"It's that damned daughter of yours!" he snarled.

"Anne—eh?" Mr. Henry Walton swore again under his breath. "Well, I had an idea it was something like that from the moment I heard the row. Come out here now and stand in the doorway, and look as bewildered as the rest of these aimless idiots! Understand? You don't know any more than they do. The shots came from somewhere around here, but that's all you can say about it."

"I'm on!" said Monsieur Faradeau.

The two men stepped out into the alleyway. Mr. Faradeau became the most excited of the figures that had gathered now in a group not far from his room. Everybody asked everybody else questions. Monsieur Faradeau indulged in a flood of exquisite French oaths, violent gesticulations, and helpless shrugs of his shoulders.

"Name of a name, the shots had seemed to ring in his very ears!

He had opened his door. Nothing was to be seen. Nothing! Monsieur Walton had been the first to arrive. *Sacré nom d'un sac au papier!* Nothing!"

A moment later the two men stood silently apart. "Well?" prompted Mr. Henry Walton in guarded tones. "Quick now!"

"She fell for that stuff you handed out at the table, and fell hard." Monsieur Faradeau spoke rapidly though his lips scarcely moved. "She came to warn me—wanted me to put the paper in the captain's safe. I had her going, all right. Made her believe she had made a mistake. And then, for some reason or other, she suddenly switched on the light and spotted that cap she knocked off the table at the bungalow last night. It was all up then, and she had me covered with a revolver like a flash. I had to come across or she would have shot me cold. She's a she-devil, and—"

"You told her Lane had the paper?" Mr. Henry Walton cut in swiftly, his eyes narrowing.

"Damn it, why shouldn't I?" returned Monsieur Faradeau as swiftly. "Yes, I told her. It was that or a bullet. You said she could be depended upon to keep her word, which would mean that she wouldn't give the show away to Lane or any one else; and, besides, the chance of something like this happening was one of the reasons why we turned the paper over to Lane anyway."

"We'll discuss that later," said Mr. Henry Walton brusquely. "What happened then?"

"She locked me in the cabin and then went out and fired all those shots and made all that row in the alleyway here."

"Which explains everything," said Mr. Henry Walton tersely. "She wouldn't break her word by giving the show away, as you put it, to Lane—but she'd *take* the paper from him if she could. That's what she made the row for—to get everybody out of their cabins—so she could get into Lane's."

Monsieur Faradeau nodded his head. An ugly look came into his face.

"Yes," he said.

"She's probably got it by now," said Mr. Henry Walton evenly; "but we're a long way from being badly hurt yet, for Lane himself is as good as the paper if you handle him right. Find him now at once. Spin him any yarn you like, so long as you get it over that all this has frightened you about the safety of the paper. Go to his stateroom with him and see if it's gone. I'll be outside. You can let me know. If it's gone, see that Lane keeps his mouth shut about it. You know the game—fix it up that the play you and Lane must make is to pretend ignorance of its loss—thief will have to disclose himself to John Crane, and get caught, and all that. I'll take care of Anne!"

"I get you!" grunted Monsieur Faradeau. "And then, of course, Lane'll come through and back me up to a finish with Crane!"

"Naturally—under the circumstances," murmured Mr. Henry Walton. "There he is over there. Go on—hurry up! There's always a chance she hasn't been able to get it."

The excitement had not abated—Captain Croon, indeed, had added to it, by suddenly appearing in his official capacity upon the scene.

Monsieur Faradeau touched Donald Lane on the shoulder, and drew him aside.

"Monsieur Lane," he whispered tremulously, "I am alarmed. I am frightened. The paper, monsieur! I am mad with fear. Let us go at once to your cabin—I beg of you, monsieur!—let us go at once to make sure that it is safe."

Donald Lane stared blankly, but allowed himself to be hurried off in the direction of his stateroom.

"What do you mean?" he demanded, as they went along. "Why the paper? The shots weren't fired at you, were they? You were not attacked in your cabin, or anything like that, were you? I heard you say you did not know anything more about it than any of the rest of us."

"And all that is true, monsieur," said Monsieur Faradeau with almost pathetic earnestness; "but still I am weak with fear. No one knows what all this is for, and nobody has seen any one, and nobody has been shot—but it is all for *something,* monsieur. And what is aboard here so valuable as my paper? And have I not been followed already half across the world? Oh, *mon Dieu,* let us make sure it is safe!"

"Right!" said Donald Lane calmly. "But don't get excited about it. It's not in the least bit likely. How could it be? No one knows I've got it. However, here we are, and we'll set your mind at rest in a jiffy."

Donald Lane had left the light in his stateroom burning. They entered, and Lane, closing the door behind them, went at once to the suit of clothes he had been wearing that evening, and secured his pocketbook.

"All right, so far, you see!" he smiled.

He opened the pocketbook, looked through it hastily, then again more carefully—and a startled look came into his face.

"Good Lord!" he gasped. "You're right! It's gone!"

Monsieur Faradeau stretched out a pair of trembling hands.

"Gone!" he echoed hoarsely. *"Mon Dieu,* I was afraid—all the time, from the first, I was afraid! Something here, inside of me"—his hand was beating nervously at his breast now—"told me it was so. But are you sure? Look—look again—for the pity of heaven, look again!"

Donald Lane once more searched through his pocketbook, this time emptying it of its contents.

"It's gone, right enough!" he said finally. Monsieur Faradeau sat down on the edge of the bunk, and covered his face with his hands.

"My God, what shall I do?" he moaned. "This is ruin—disaster—and not, monsieur, for myself alone, but for all those others."

Donald Lane's face had set grimly.

"Not yet, it isn't!" he said tersely. "And under the circumstances I do not see how it is going to do the thief any good."

Monsieur Faradeau looked up.

"How do you mean?" he asked anxiously. "Simply that, having seen the paper," replied Donald Lane, "and knowing that it is the one in my uncle's handwriting, I have only to vouch for that fact to my uncle, and for you personally as the one who placed it in my hands for safe-keeping. You may be quite certain that the package will be turned over to no one else but yourself."

"You will do that, monsieur!" Monsieur Faradeau rose excitedly to his feet.

"Naturally!" returned Donald Lane calmly. "What else could I do? I am to blame now, if any one is. I should have taken greater precaution to hide the paper, having once accepted it from you. But you need have no concern in so far as the theft of the paper affects you. That, however, does not let the thief out—and I don't mind saying I'd like to get my hands on him."

"Yes!" exclaimed Monsieur Faradeau fervently. *"Mon Dieu,* yes—even to know who it is! To put an end to this espionage that for weeks has made of me almost a crazy man!"

Donald Lane's brows had furrowed suddenly.

"How the devil did he know I had the paper?" he ejaculated.

"In only one way," said Monsieur Faradeau heavily. "We must have been seen together on the deck. I must have been seen going to monsieur's stateroom, and—and we must have been overheard."

Donald Lane nodded.

"I suppose so," he agreed. "Well, what shall we do? Go out there and tell the captain? Have everybody on board searched for the paper? It sounds a bit hopeless."

Monsieur Faradeau shook his head.

"It would be worse than hopeless. We have no —what do you call it?—a clue?—to work upon. Nothing! It is the thief himself who must—what do you call it again?—make the next play. And we must watch."

"Yes," said Lane in a puzzled tone, "I agree with you in that; but I must confess I still do not see his game. What's the good of the paper to him? He couldn't go to my uncle with it in Talimi when he had stolen it from me, and you are also there to claim it as your property. It's a bit queer, I'll say!"

Monsieur Faradeau was not without guile.

"No, monsieur"—Monsieur Faradeau lowered his voice—"I am afraid it is not queer, but that it is very serious—*very* serious, monsieur—for both monsieur and for me. He has got the paper now, and, as monsieur says, it is useless, worth nothing to him when our story is told to Monsieur Crane, for monsieur is good enough to say that he will see that I get the package—but what if *neither of us* is at Talimi, when the thief presents the paper to Monsieur Crane?"

"What!" ejaculated Lane. "You mean—"

"Yes, monsieur"—Monsieur Faradeau nodded his head gravely again—"there may be only one of them here on this ship, there may be more—I do not know. But I know they will stop at nothing, that murder means nothing to them; and I know that if neither monsieur nor myself is at Talimi, Monsieur Crane will deliver that package to whoever delivers that paper to Monsieur Crane. Is it not so, monsieur?"

Donald Lane whistled low under his breath.

"That's a pleasant thought!" he exclaimed. "The idea, then, of all this row up forward was simply to get *me* to leave my cabin here!"

Monsieur Faradeau nodded silently.

Donald Lane paced several times up and down the length of the stateroom, and then halted before Monsieur Faradeau again.

"I don't believe you've hit it at all," he said abruptly. "There's something more back of this. The thief isn't fool enough to have gone to the length he has unless he was reasonably sure he could make use of the paper once it was in his possession —and the theory that he would still have to murder both of us to accomplish his purpose is a little bit more than I can believe." His face was suddenly set and stern. "We'll see this thing through—to a showdown! We are both agreed that it would do no good to make the theft of the paper public in so far as getting it back is concerned; but there is another reason, if I am right in believing there's a deeper game being played, why we should say nothing for the moment. We would only put the thief on his guard. Between the row out there and the theft of the paper there is apparently no connection—we'll give the thief credit for being clever enough in that. If we say nothing, he may imagine —and I rather fancy that's what he is counting on—that it has never occurred to me to look in my pocketbook to see if the paper is safe, and that I might even land at Talimi without any suspicion that the paper was gone. You understand?"

Monsieur Faradeau *quite* understood! As Monsieur Faradeau had rather expected, Donald Lane had clamped his jaws, much after the fashion of a dog with a bone in its mouth, over the hint of personal danger, with the result that Donald Lane had now assumed the initiative in formulating a plan of action precisely along the lines Monsieur Faradeau most earnestly desired. Not for worlds would Monsieur Faradeau by word or sign have attempted to retrieve the leading role!

"Yes!" said Monsieur Faradeau with sudden eagerness. "*Bon Dieu*—yes! I did not think of that!"

"Very well!" Lane smiled grimly. "As a matter of fact I'm rather curious, even at the cost of a little personal risk, to see what he'll do. As you said, and you hit it there, right enough, it's his next play. Well, we'll give him all the line he wants—without tugging on it until he's hooked! He has certainly got to be caught at no matter what risk, for, otherwise, he will still be on your trail when you leave Talimi, and when you have, not merely the paper, but the actual package itself in your possession."

Monsieur Faradeau ran his hand nervously through his hair.

"You are right, monsieur—a thousand times right!" he cried out. "Yes, that is what we will do! We will say nothing—not a word. We will pretend that we do not know that our paper has been taken. And we will watch—and, *nom d'un sacré nom,* we will get our fingers on his throat. But meanwhile I think that monsieur and I should—how do you say it?—keep guard on each other, monsieur. For me, I am never without a revolver under my pillow or in my pocket, and I beg that monsieur will now do the same."

"Yes; I rather think I will," said Lane laconically.

"I am glad!" said Monsieur Faradeau in a relieved tone of voice. "It is good—I cannot tell monsieur how good of him it is to share the risk with me—and I shall feel safer for his sake to know always that he is armed. And now, monsieur, while they are still excited out there—*tonnerre,* listen to the talk!—I will slip out."

"All right," said Lane. "I'll follow in a moment, and hang around for a bit."

Monsieur Faradeau opened the door of the cabin cautiously, slipped out cautiously, and cautiously closed the door behind him.

Mr. Henry Walton, curiously enough, slipped out of his cabin next door at the same instant.

A little further along the alleyway were several small, chattering and still excited groups of passengers.

Monsieur Faradeau passed Mr. Henry Walton without stopping or even glancing in the other's direction.

"She pinched it—but it's a cinch," said the polished "Frenchman" out of the corner of his mouth. "Go as far as you like!"

ANNE had switched on the light in her stateroom. Her face was flushed, her breath was still coming in quick, painful little gasps. Her father would be here in a moment—as soon as his accomplice, the so-called Monsieur Faradeau, had been able to tell him what had happened. She expected that—that was what she was waiting for now—these were the consequences. But she had the paper, and the package was safe—there wouldn't be any crime committed—John Crane would not be robbed. Her father must *see* the paper—and then she would tear it up, destroy it before his eyes—and—and accept the consequences. It would be better, safer, for whoever was to redeem the package that he should go back to Paris empty-handed. Eventually those to whom it belonged would get it—but her father and his accomplice, when that time came, would no longer be a menace.

A hubbub of voices, movement, still came from up forward in the direction of the saloon.

Her door opened and closed suddenly.

Her father faced her—his back against the door.

She saw his eyes behind their amber-coloured glasses fix first on the paper, and then on the revolver which she held in the other hand.

His lips parted in a cool smile.

"I see, my dear Anne," he said suavely, "that you have got it."

"Yes," she said steadily; "I have got it. And I want you to be quite *sure* that I've got it." She held up the slip of paper unfolded—but well out of his reach. "Are you satisfied that this is it?"

"Oh, quite!" said Henry Walton. "And now that you've got it, would it be too much to ask what you propose to do with it?"

"I am going to destroy it," Anne answered in a level voice; "here, now, in front of you!"

"Really!" Henry Walton shook his head tolerantly. "How impetuous you are, Anne! Listen to the proof of it out there! What a disturbance that unfortunate trait of yours—your besetting sin, my dear, I think I might call it—has already caused to-night!"

Anne made no answer—but suddenly bringing her two hands together, while still pointing the revolver at her father, she tore the slip of paper in two. Then mechanically she retreated a pace, expecting some effort on his part to interfere. He made none. She tore the slip across once more; and then quickly, almost frantically,

120

reduced the paper to little shreds.

"I would suggest the port-hole as a final depository," said Mr. Walton casually.

Anne stared at him. Her face paled a little. His attitude of utter nonchalance brought her a sudden and disturbing sense of dismay. And then her shoulders straightened defiantly, and she stepped quickly across the cabin.

"That is exactly what I am going to do," she said —and let the pieces flutter out from her hand through the open port-hole.

Henry Walton nodded approvingly.

"Under the circumstances," he drawled, "I would have destroyed it myself if you had not so obligingly done it for me. It would have been a little awkward, once it was stolen, to account for the reappearance of the paper."

"What do you mean?" she demanded tensely.

Henry Walton shrugged his shoulders; his cool smile broadened.

"My dear Anne," he said apologetically, "I am afraid that the details of the little story I told you last night were not wholly accurate in some instances. The man who originally set out from Paris with that paper—er—disappeared some time ago, and—er—his place was taken by my friend Monsieur Faradeau, who has just been honoured with a call from you at—really, Anne!—a rather unseasonable hour for young ladies to be about. Monsieur Faradeau and myself are quite alone in this little matter."

"Alone!" she said in a low voice. "Yes, I can see that; you—you got rid of the man who originally carried the paper. But—Donald! I—I don't understand. Donald had the paper."

"My dear," said Henry Walton softly, "you will learn—if you live long enough—that it is always prudent to have something in reserve against the unexpected which so often arises. One never knows! Er—I believe you may have heard that expression? But one is a fool who shuts his eyes to an opportunity that in any degree forearms him against possible mishap. Something *might* happen to that paper. I even suspected that *you* might attempt something, though, if you did, it would only be with Monsieur Faradeau, and only to inform us exactly of your movements—thanks to that little dinner-table conversation in which I noticed you were so wholly absorbed. But, quite apart from all that, Monsieur Faradeau, with his credentials indorsed by Mr. John Crane's nephew, would be in so impregnable a position when he presented himself at Talimi as having come from Mr. Todd in Paris, that it was very much worth while using Mr. Lane for that purpose alone. I am sure you see that, Anne?"

Yes; she was beginning to see! Her face was white.

"Go on!" she said almost inaudibly.

"The rest is rather obvious," said Henry Walton. "At my suggestion, Monsieur Faradeau went to Donald Lane and told him the story with all its fears and hopes, just as I imagine the—er—the one who originally started out from Paris might have told it, and Mr. Lane very kindly consented to take charge of the document in question until Talimi was reached. Monsieur Faradeau's fears *were* realized—but you will appreciate the result, Anne! Monsieur Faradeau obviously will say nothing of *your* visit to his room, not—er—even to Mr. Lane; nobody will know what all the disturbance could possibly have been about—except Donald Lane and Monsieur Faradeau, who, ingeniously putting two and two together, will realize that it was caused by *some one* in order to steal that paper. And since I am sure, Anne, that you will not violate your pledge, you will not say anything about it either. Monsieur Faradeau and Mr. Lane will consult with each other as to what is best to be done. Their conclusion is apparent. They will say nothing on board here about the theft. At Talimi, Mr. Lane will introduce Monsieur Faradeau to his uncle, explain the circumstances, vouch for Monsieur Faradeau, and vouch for the fact that the paper was in John Crane's handwriting; John Crane will hand over the package to Monsieur Faradeau, and they will all wait for the thug to show his hand with the stolen paper —and wonder why he doesn't. You can quite understand, therefore, the—er—lack of necessity of that paper coming to light again; and also why, under the circumstances, it is much better destroyed. It would be so difficult for Monsieur Faradeau to explain if it were returned to him; and so apt to arouse Mr. Lane's suspicions if it were returned to—Mr. Lane!"

Mr. Walton paused, searched for his cigarette case, opened it, and carefully selected a cigarette.

"Will you permit me, Anne?" he murmured softly.

Anne's shoulders had drooped a little; the revolver hung listlessly in her hand. Dismal, utter failure stared her in the face. She had not only accomplished nothing, she had made matters worse— made success now, apparently, an impossibility. A great weight, from under which she was mentally impotent to rise, seemed to be crushing her down; it seemed to rob her of the spirit to fight any longer even with words. She wanted to fling herself down on the bunk there, and bury her face in the pillow.

She made no reply.

"Thank you so much!" Henry Walton murmured again in the same soft tones. "I think I said last night that, knowing you would keep strictly within the limits of your pledge, any little personal role you attempted to play would inject a very welcome touch of amusement into the affair! But I mustn't keep you up. You must be very tired, my dear. Good-night, Anne!"

The door opened and closed behind him.

She heard her father's voice raised above those of several others just outside her door:

"Yes, most extraordinary! Nobody seems to be able to make head or tail of it! I was just reassuring my daughter by telling her that at least no accident had happened to the ship, and that there was no danger. Most amazing!"

For a time Anne did not move; then suddenly the drooping shoulders lifted, and she stood erect, her head thrown back, her white face set, her eyes shining, tearless.

"I'm not beaten!" she whispered passionately. "I'm not! I'm not! I'm not!"

CHAPTER XI   THE ONLY DOOR LEFT OPEN

FROM her cabin port-hole Anne could see a fringe of palms against the sky line, a little row of white houses peeping through heavy, green foliage, and a long white stretch of beach that glistened in the sunlight. It was Kaliti, a little island that she knew very well and had visited many times, for it was one of the Talimi group and hardly more than twenty miles from Talimi itself.

From forward she heard the rattle of the *Alola's* steam winch, as the vessel prepared to drop anchor. It was almost five o'clock in the afternoon now. The *Alola* would stay here perhaps an hour to unload whatever freight she had for the little place, and then go on to Talimi. Talimi would be reached somewhere about half-past nine that evening—after dark.

Anne's face was very grave, and tears were not far from her eyes. It seemed as though it were a miserable thing she was about to do—a sort of betrayal—to make use of a man's love—to play a siren's part! Her small hands clenched. But there was no other way. She must go on.

She had not been on deck, she had not left her stateroom since last night; she had waited for Kaliti —because she knew Kaliti, and—and some of those who lived there.

From the moment her father had left the stateroom after she had torn up the paper, she had been faced with one final, desperate chance; there was only one, and it was a very obvious one—the package itself! To get the package itself! Given the opportunity to get into John Crane's house, she was almost certain she could find it. In those old girlhood days, so long ago now, she had known the house as intimately as she knew her own. There had been no safe in the house then; and she was quite sure none had been installed since. She would have heard of it otherwise. That was the kind of thing the natives would chatter about, and the kind of thing that would furnish a topic for small talk among the whites.

The memory of the "doll's house" had come back to her with startling significance—that panel in the living-room wall which used to open and shut so mysteriously until the day when, watching very closely, she had seen John Crane press on a certain spot under the mantel, and, clapping her hands in delight, she, too, had made the panel slide back—a little to his consternation. And significant, too, now seemed the very serious way in which he had warned her never to say anything about it to any one, impressing on her young mind the fact that "doll's house" was only "play," and that it was really there to preserve certain valuables from the light-fingered natives who might be tempted to steal.

She was sure the package was in the "doll's house"—sure as one is sometimes sure of things without having any concrete reason for being sure, and yet so sure that one feels one *knows*.

But the belief, however well-founded, that she knew where the package was, and the resolve to get it before it came into the possession of her father and his confederate in crime, was quite another matter from determining how her purpose could be accomplished. The *Alola* would be at Talimi that evening; and, the moment they landed, the man who called himself Faradeau, accompanied by Donald, would go to John Crane; Donald would vouch for the other, and John Crane would deliver the package to Monsieur Faradeau. That was exactly what would happen unless it could be prevented.

The most obvious move she could make would be to get to John Crane's house *first*—and she believed she knew how she could get away from the *Alola*, not only unseen, but before anybody else did. But she did not dare depend on that alone. It would take so little to prevent her leaving the ship the way she planned—and then, even if she were successful in reaching John Crane's house first, she would have only a very few minutes before the others arrived; and, besides, though the household would customarily be down to meet the *Alola*, some one might still be about, and she would not be able to employ those few minutes in searching even the "doll's house;" and then again, the package might not be in the "doll's house" at all, and those "few minutes" would then be utterly worthless to her. In any case she meant to try out this plan because it was obviously the quickest and safest way—but it was far too uncertain of success to permit her to stake everything upon it. She must in some way make it absolutely certain that, if she failed in this first attempt, she would still be left with an opportunity to search for the package before it was removed or handed over to her father's accomplice.

It was this phase of the problem that had tortured her brain for hours. And then, perhaps by suggestion, but logically enough, the answer had come. Without that paper and without Donald Lane to vouch for him, Monsieur Faradeau would certainly not get the package, or even attempt to get it, from John Crane. If Donald, then, could be *marooned,* as her father had led her to believe some one else was to be marooned, and for essentially the same purpose, it would give her, in the sense of time at least, the opportunity she would require if her first attempt were a failure. It would give her the *night.* It was much more difficult and dangerous—she knew that. She would not only have to steal away from her own house, but find an entrance into John Crane's without awakening anybody. But it was *all* difficult and dangerous. And —and that did not matter any more.

The steam winch clattered noisily. She heard the rattle of the chain as the anchor went overside. Her brows drew together. She must hurry! The native boats would already be alongside, and the gangway would be down in a minute. She reached quickly into the recesses of a handbag and took out a letter she had written that morning. She glanced at the envelope a little askance. It was addressed to "Donald Lane, Esq." Her lips firmed. She thrust the letter hurriedly into the bodice of her dress, made her way quickly on deck, and crossing to the rail, stood leaning over, apparently engrossed now in no other thing in the world than the natives with their boats and outrigger canoes who swarmed around the ship's side below.

Her heart was beating wildly.

Up forward under the bridge, Donald Lane was chatting with a little group of passengers. She saw him leave his companions and start hurriedly in her direction.

Another moment and he was standing beside her. Her knees seemed suddenly to be miserably weak— her hands tightened on the rail. She forced herself to look up smilingly.

"Mr. Lane!" she exclaimed pleasantly.

"Miss Walton—Anne," he said as though she had not spoken, a strange hoarseness in his voice, "what is the matter?"

"Matter?" She was still smiling as she echoed the word inquiringly. *"Is* there anything the matter, Mr. Lane?"

"There is all the matter in the world!" His tones were low, shaken now, as he leaned quickly toward her. "Yesterday I—I did not understand at all. I was to go for you to the bungalow. And on board here you have studiously avoided me!"

"I—I'm sorry," said Anne, "if I have made you feel that I was avoiding you; but"—one hand left the rail, and, hidden at her side,

clenched until the nails biting at the flesh gave her physical hurt—
"but, at least, I am not avoiding you now, am I? I was just going
ashore for a little while—we'll be here an hour or more, you know.
Would you care to come?"

"Oh, may I?" he cried eagerly.

"Of course!" said Anne—and led the way to the gangway.

She passed her father on the deck.

"Going ashore, Anne?" he asked.

"Yes," she answered briefly.

"And you, too, eh, Lane?" said Henry Walton with a bland smile.
"A very pretty place—Kaliti!" He clapped Lane in friendly fashion
upon the shoulder. "I think you're quite safe this time," he laughed;
"the barometer is rising."

Anne went down the gangway and seated herself in a boat
manned by four natives. Her father wasn't suspicious—couldn't be.
Donald Lane no longer had the paper that, otherwise, by cajolery or
theft, her father might have feared she would be able to obtain. What
her father might think later, when the *Alola* sailed again, was another
matter—probably he would be annoyed, though still hardly
suspicious—but it wouldn't matter then—it would be too late.

Donald Lane took his place beside her.

She searched her mind frantically for some topic of conversation.

"Look!" she said, as the boat pulled away from the ship. "In clear
weather like this you can just barely see Talimi from here." She
pointed to what seemed like a tiny spot of haze on the surface of the
water far away to the eastward. "It's because Talimi's hilly, I
suppose, that one can see it, though it's only about twenty miles away.
Isn't it strange, the difference in these islands? Kaliti here is very
beautiful, but it is almost absolutely flat."

Lane's dark eyes held her face steadily.

"I have been looking at Talimi with a great longing for more than
two weeks now—ever since a certain ship came to Suva from
Auckland," he said gravely.

Her hand trailed in the water. She made no answer.

"Anne, what is the matter?" he asked again. "What have I done?"

She had invited it. It had to come. In one way she *wanted* it to
come—it was far better that it should. But not yet—not here in the
boat with these four native boys staring at her. And—and, besides,
there was something she must do first ashore, and for which she might

not have the courage afterwards.

"You have not done anything," she said in a low voice; "but do not let us talk here. Wait till we get ashore. I"—she smiled up at him suddenly—"I have decided that you are going to take me for a drive."

"Of course!" His face broke instantly into a quick, eager smile. "That is, provided anything can be found to drive in."

"There will be no trouble about that," said Anne —and again her head was turned away. She despised herself—hated herself. She had become very proficient in the art of deception. It was necessary that a conveyance of some kind should already be in his possession when, later on, the *Alola* sailed and he remained behind; otherwise, his explanations then of why he wanted one might very easily bring in their wake information that would at once arouse his suspicions—in time perhaps even to enable him still to catch the *Alola* before the ship got under way. "You can always get an animal and a buggy, such as they are, at Willett's."

"Fine!" said Lane enthusiastically.

The boat had covered the short distance from the ship; it grounded now on the beach. As they stepped ashore, Anne pointed to one of the little group of buildings that, straggling out along the road some fifty yards or so from the beach, comprised the town.

"That's Willett's," she said; "the one with the new piece of galvanized iron that looks like a spangle on the roof. If you will go ahead and get the horse, I will meet you in front of the store—I want to go in there for a moment."

"Right!" said Lane. "But don't you be long— we've only an hour!"

She watched him as he hurried away—and suddenly she brushed her hand across her eyes. But her head was up in an instant, and she, too, started toward the road. She knew Kaliti well—she had known it since babyhood. Here and there a native saluted her with a wide grin and childlike delight. Anne of Talimi, as she was called in the neighbouring islands, was equally well known herself. She halted one of the natives, as though for a more extended greeting than a mere passing smile of recognition, and pointed down the road to Donald Lane's retreating figure.

She spoke rapidly in the native tongue.

The man nodded.

Anne drew out the letter and handed it, together with some

money from her purse, to the other.

Again she spoke rapidly, earnestly; and again the man nodded as he tucked the letter inside his *lava-lava.*

She turned away and went on toward the store— but the parting, radiant smile for her trusting native dupe was gone. Her lips were quivering like a child's on the verge of tears.

CHAPTER XII   MAN AND MAID

ANNE entered the one general store that supplied the needs of the entire island, made a small, inconsequential purchase, and was standing outside again as Donald Lane drove up with the horse and buggy.

"Not bad!" he called out. "Seems like a very decent beast. Wait till I help you climb in!"

There was something quiet, firm in his grasp as he took her hand and arm; a sense of *masterfulness* in his touch, as though having at last possessed himself of that which he desired he thereafter proposed to keep it. She felt this; she saw it in his steady smile. Her face flushed a little.

They drove off—and at first in silence. The road, once away from the town, was like a shady lane, twisting and turning charmingly through a little forest of tropical trees and plants, cool and fragrant with the odours of fruits and blossoms.

An hour! She must keep him for an hour—until just before the *Alola* sailed. It was the *last* hour she would ever be with him. She was smiling, wasn't she; and her face was composed; and she appeared to be quite at ease—didn't she? She wondered how it could be possible when there was so great a turmoil in her soul and her heart was beating so furiously that it made sounds like dull hammer blows in her ears. An hour! If that could only span the rest of all her life! She shivered slightly. Time would soften memories for him— if contempt did not at once obliterate them! It would be different with her. She would love this man always, live his life with him in her thoughts, no matter where he was, hope for his happiness and his joys, pray for him always. But here in this hour was the end between them. If she succeeded in what she was risking all for now, she would steal away from Talimi on the *Alola* when the ship sailed the next morning (Captain Croon had said at daybreak), and she would be gone when Donald reached the island again.

She was conscious that he was studying her face earnestly. She nerved herself to force conversation. Last night on the *Alola!* Nothing could be more natural than to speak of that; it was so naturally one of the first things on the tip of one's tongue, and especially of hers, the only woman passenger on board, that it would be most strange if she did not refer to it.

"Have you heard anything more about the disturbance on board last night?" she asked. "Has any one discovered what it was all about?"

He did not answer for a moment, and she saw a shadow cross his face.

"I wish you had not asked that, Anne," he said at last. "To anybody else I would lie promptly and say no; but, as a matter of fact, I do know what the cause of it was, though I do not know who caused it."

"Oh!" she said a little faintly. "I—I didn't mean to invite confidences."

"You will never invite them," he answered; "they are yours always when I am free to give them. I can't tell you anything about it now; but to-morrow, perhaps, or, anyway, some time when we are back in Talimi I will tell you the whole story."

She wanted to laugh out loudly—not in mirth, but in an hysterical effort to find relief from pent-up emotions. *He* would tell her the story—the man who had been made a cat's-paw to serve her father's criminal ends! He who, even at this moment, she herself was planning to deceive! She wished now she had never mentioned the subject.

They drove for a little while again in silence, and presently she noticed that he kept glancing intently from first one side of the road to the other.

"What is it?" she asked. "What are you looking for?"

"For a little dell—as nearly like a certain one on the hills of Fiji as I can find," he answered quietly.

She laughed nervously.

"But surely," she cried, and tried to force a note of banter into her voice, "you wouldn't want a repetition of that afternoon—or any more 'thunderstorms!' "

"No," he said, "not in that way; but there will be just the two of us together again—alone." He turned the horse suddenly off the road into a little grove of trees. "I think this will do. There isn't any stream here; just the cool shade, and the flowers, and the sweet smells of growing things— but there isn't time to search further." His voice broke a little. "We—we've only a very short time, just a few minutes before we have to go back again. Croon said he had very little for the island, and would sail promptly in an hour. Won't you get out, Anne?"

She made no protest, as he took her arm and helped her to alight. The colour was coming and going in her face; she knew it, knew that he saw it —and yet she passively allowed him to lead her a little farther in amongst the trees away from the road.

And then he halted, and took her hand, and for the third time asked the same question:

"What is the matter, Anne?"

She shook her head.

"Nothing," she answered.

"That afternoon, Anne," he said, as though he had not heard her reply, "you saved my life at the risk of your own, and afterwards when you were ill you said things that—"

She had a role to play. She was not playing it. She forced herself to draw back a little—to free her hand.

"One is not responsible for what one says in— in delirium," she interrupted.

"No; but it is rather good evidence of what is passing in one's mind," he said quietly. "And then you wrote me a note. And, after what had previously passed between us, if ever a woman told a man she loved him, you told me so in that note."

Anne laughed a little harshly.

"Yes," she said; "perhaps I was a little indiscreet."

"Indiscreet!" he cried. "You *cared!* You gave me my answer— the answer that meant everything in life I hoped for. But since then something has happened. You could not have acted as you did if you had not cared."

"Well, since you insist on knowing," said Anne very steadily, "I am afraid I allowed myself to be carried away when I wrote that note; but—you know—there is always the woman's prerogative."

"Ah!" he cried out eagerly. "You admit then, since you claim the right to change your mind, that you *did* love me!"

She braced herself with a great mental effort.

She was fighting—for his sake—for the contempt of the man she loved.

"No," she said coolly. "I admit—a passing whim."

He drew back as though she had struck him a blow across the face. His lips were white, set.

"I do not believe you!" he said hoarsely.

Anne leaned back against a tree-trunk—something seemed to be draining her physical strength away. She shrugged her shoulders calmly.

"I am afraid you will have to," she said.

"I do not believe you!" he repeated even more vehemently. "You are not that kind of a woman. You couldn't play with a man! If you cared once, you cared for always. Anne, you loved me then— and you love me now!"

A surge of longing, of intense yearning swept over her. She wanted to raise her hands and smooth away those hurt lines around his lips, and drive the agony out of his face, and—and hold that bandaged head upon her bosom, and comfort him.

"No, I do not love you," she said in a level voice.

He leaned toward her suddenly and caught her by the shoulders.

"Look at me!" he ordered.

She raised her eyes, met his for a moment, tried to hold his gaze—and with a quick, broken, little cry turned her head away.

"*Anne!* I saw it there! The light! The love-light! You *do* love me!" he cried passionately— and swept her into his arms. "Anne! Anne! I read it there in your eyes—they cannot lie!"

"Oh, don't! Please!" she pleaded wildly—and tried to free herself. "Have mercy! You do not know what you are doing!"

"No!" he answered back. "You are mine, Anne, mine! I know it now!"

For a moment she struggled feverishly to cover her face with her hands, fighting back the kisses that he showered upon her eyes, her lips, her hair; and then, as though all her strength were gone, she lay quiet in his embrace—and a great joy thrilled her. It was just for a moment, a glimpse into a world that wasn't hers—a world of love— his love. And her heart cried out to him to hold her closer, tighter to him, to hold her there always—but her lips moaned.

He let her go after a little while, and she sank down at the foot of the tree and hid her face in her hands.

"Oh, what have you done!" she cried out miserably.

He was on his knees beside her, his arm around her shoulders.

"What have I done?" His voice came in triumphant little gasps. "What have I done? I've proved that you love me!"

"Then—then so much the worse for you—and me," she said brokenly.

"What do you mean?" he asked.

"I mean," she said, "that—that even if I loved you, there—there can never be anything between us."

"Why not?" he demanded, and there was a sudden challenge in his voice. "It's that infernal row between your father and my uncle that's cropped up again!"

"No," Anne answered, and rose a little unsteadily to her feet. "It's—it's because I am not what you think I am. I have no right to your love."

For a moment he stared at her in a sort of numbed amazement.

"I—I don't understand," he said.

"And I cannot tell you any more," she said. "Won't you please take me back to the beach? It must be nearly time for the *Alola* to sail."

"No right!" he burst out fiercely. "I do not know what you mean—but there isn't anything, no matter what it is, that shall come between us!"

"Something has already come—something that neither you nor I can ever overcome," Anne answered with averted face.

She made a step forward toward the road, but he blocked the way.

"Anne, you shall not go like this! You shall not! I must know what it is! Tell me! Trust me! Our love is bigger, stronger, than anything that is frightening you so!"

"You—you are making it very hard," she said, "for I can never tell you." Her eyes were full of tears. "Won't you please take me back now?"

For an instant he hesitated, then quietly he led her back to the road and helped her into the buggy.

"For the moment, yes, Anne," he said with forced composure. "We won't say anything more about it now. You are overwrought. And I'm afraid I've been a bit of a brute. We'll leave it, shall we, for the days ahead at Talimi? And thank God for those days—for I shall never let you go!"

She did not reply; nor did he speak again until near the little town, when the hoarse blast of a steamer's whistle reached their ears.

"We've just timed it nicely," said Lane, with an attempt at lightness.

"Yes," Anne answered.

Her faced had paled a little.

134

Running toward them, as they came in sight of the beach, was a native who carried a letter in his hand.

Lane reined in the horse and took the envelope.

The man spoke volubly, with many gesticulations.

"What does he say?" Lane asked.

"He says he got here too late to catch you when the *Alola* came in," Anne said, fighting with every word to speak calmly; "and that he has been trying to find you ever since."

Lane tore the envelope open, and rapidly read the contents.

"Confound it!" he exclaimed. "What a beastly nuisance!" He dug into his pockets for a piece of money and dismissed the native. "I'm afraid I shall have to stay over here to-night. This a letter from a chap named Thompson, or, rather, from his wife—do you happen to know them? I don't!"

"Oh, yes!" said Anne. "Mr. Thompson has quite a large plantation on the other side of the island. The road we were on takes you there. It's about an hour from here."

Lane nodded.

"Mrs. Thompson says her husband is down with a touch of dengue fever, which accounts for her writing, and for the fact that, otherwise, Mr. Thompson would have driven in for me. She says my uncle was over here last week on some business with her husband, some inventory of Thompson's copra, I take it, that he was going to turn over to us, and that wasn't completed; and that my uncle suggested I should stay over when the *Alola* reached here and check up Thompson's figures, and so save the double trip—and that my uncle would send for me the next day."

"I see," said Anne, without looking up.

"I'll have to write a note to Croon, I suppose," said Lane, frowning thoughtfully, "and tell him to have one of the stewards pack up my gear and put it ashore at Talimi. There's no time for anything else—and besides, of course, the stuff would be a bother here."

"There's Captain Croon down there on the beach now," said Anne.

They both got out of the buggy and went down to one of the shore boats in which the *Alola's* skipper was preparing to embark.

Lane explained the letter he had received, and made his request anent his baggage—and then drew Captain Croon a little to one side.

"Look here," he said, "tell Monsieur Faradeau quietly from me to introduce himself to my uncle, and that I'll be along some time to-morrow."

"Right, you are!" agreed Captain Croon genially. Then to Anne: "Hop in, Miss Anne, and come out with me."

Anne held out her hand to Donald Lane.

"Good-bye," she said.

He smiled at her steadily.

"Until to-morrow!" he answered in a low tone.

Anne stepped into the boat; and, presently, she found herself climbing the *Alola's* gangway. And then, standing on the deck, she looked shoreward. Through a mist which suddenly dimmed her eyes she saw a figure that she never expected to see again—a figure in white, with bandaged head, that stood upon the beach and waved a pith helmet in farewell.

CHAPTER XIII   MAROONED

IT was an hour later when, on the other side of of Kaliti, Lane drove up to a large and substantial looking house that, facing the beach, was set back a short distance from the road. A man of middle age, a stocky figure in riding breeches, with shirt open at the neck, came courteously forward from the verandah to meet him.

"My name's Lane," said Donald Lane pleasantly. "I'm John Crane's nephew. I wonder if you'd be good enough to let Mrs. Thompson know I've come?"

"Why—yes, certainly!" answered the man in a somewhat perplexed way. He swung around and called toward the house. "Nina! Come here a moment, will you! There's some one to see you!" He turned to Lane again, and held out his hand. "I'm Thompson," he said cordially.

Lane stared.

"Oh!" he ejaculated. He shook hands. "I expected to find you in bed. I'm glad to see you're so much better."

"Better!" said Thompson, staring hard in return. "I was never better in my life."

"But—but your wife wrote that you were down with dengue fever," said Lane a little helplessly.

"Not me!" said Thompson. "I haven't had an ache for twenty years!"

"There must be some mistake, then," said Lane. "I've got the wrong house. It's some other Thompson that I am looking for."

"Then you won't find him!" grinned the other. "I'm the only man by the name of Thompson on Kaliti."

"Well that's damned queer!" said Donald Lane. He took the letter from his pocket, and handed it to the other.

Thompson read it. He was reading it for the second time, when a matronly woman came smilingly from the house and joined them.

"My wife," said Thompson. "Nina, this is Mr. Lane—Crane of Talimi's nephew. He has brought a letter from you."

"From me!" exclaimed Mrs. Thompson. "How do you do, Mr. Lane? From me! But I—"

Thompson handed his wife the letter—and, in turn, she read it, amazement growing in her face.

"Why—why, I never wrote this!" she cried out bewilderedly.

"No," said Thompson; "and to my certain knowledge John Crane hasn't been in Kaliti in a year. I'm afraid some one has been indulging in a practical joke—though I must say it's a bit thick to make you let the *Alola* go on without you, as, I take it, is the case. However, it's an ill wind—you know. John Crane's nephew is one of the family here any time."

Lane's face hardened, whitened a little. It wasn't any joke! He saw it all in a flash now. It was the answer to why that paper had been stolen from him last night. Faradeau, after all had been right! It was obvious now that the thief *had* planned that neither Faradeau nor he, Donald Lane, should be at Talimi to interfere with the credentials being presented to John Crane. John Crane would then, of course, hand the package over at once, and the thief would make his escape with his prize on the *Alola* again—since the *Alola* would only stay a few hours, say till daybreak, at Talimi. He, Donald Lane, had been neatly and cleverly disposed of—at least temporarily. What about Faradeau? What had happened to Faradeau—or, more likely, what *would* happen to Faradeau between Kaliti and Talimi? It was just as essential to the thief's success, since the thief had now disclosed his hand and this was his game, that Faradeau should also be disposed of. In Faradeau's case would it be only *temporarily?* Faradeau had been tracked and followed from Paris; Faradeau had not hesitated to suggest the probability of a grim and sudden ending for himself—or, indeed, for both of them!

Lane's hands clenched suddenly.

"I'm afraid it's far from a joke!" he said grimly. "So far from it, that in some way or other I've got to reach Talimi as soon as the *Alola* does. And, at that, I'm afraid I can't stop what may be murder on board of her on her way over."

"Good God!" Thompson's jaw dropped. "Is it as bad as that?"

"Yes!" said Lane tersely. He was staring down at the beach where, inside a coral reef that acted as a natural breakwater, a small boat was moored to a wharf. "Isn't that a motorboat you've got there?"

"Well of a sort!" Thompson answered. "At least there's an engine in her, and she does all right for puttering around in; but ten miles an hour is the utmost she can do, and the *Alola* must have left an hour ago."

Lane figured quickly.

She left at six—it's about seven now," he said. Her best is between six or seven knots an hour. It's twenty miles to Talimi. It will take her a good three hours—that's nine o'clock. Two hours from now at ten miles an hour means Talimi—at nine o'clock. And, besides, the *Alola* would have to lose a mile or two working in through the reefs. May I have your boat, Mr. Thompson?"

"By the Lord Harry," cried Thompson bluffly, "you're John Crane's nephew, and no mistake! You bet, you may have her, and I'll send one of the native boys with you to run her. I'm not sure you'll make it, but it's a sporting chance, and, I'd say, an even break. Nina, send some one to find Ratu, while Mr. Lane and I get the boat ready. Come along Mr. Lane—we'll see that your horse gets back safely."

With a hurried adieu to Mrs. Thompson, Lane followed Thompson down to the wharf—and five minutes later, with his crew of one, he was headed out to sea in the direction of Talimi.

The craft proved to be an ordinary rowboat in which an engine had been installed, and to Lane it seemed to travel like a snail. There was little conversation—and what there was of it was understood neither by Lane nor his native companion, save when it was amplified by the common and unmistakable language of gesticulation. His efforts, for instance, to make Ratu understand that they must go faster brought only a good-natured grin and a shake of the head.

At the end of an hour it had begun to grow dark. There was no longer any land to be seen in the fading light—neither Talimi ahead nor Kaliti astern. But this did not seem in any way to disturb Ratu. Donald Lane resigned himself to such philosophical patience as he could muster. It was at least a smooth sea, and there was the promise of a moonlight night.

Last night, this afternoon with Anne, and then the letter!—his thoughts were full of conflicting emotions. But they dwelt mostly on Anne. This attempt to obtain the package, the unknown criminal hand at work, was, in one sense, so clear-cut, definite and direct in its demand for responsive action on his part that it almost automatically took care of itself. It was damnable, vicious work, and he meant to render it abortive if he could. He was doing now all that it was humanly possible to do. He could do nothing more until Talimi was reached.

But Anne! It was different with Anne! He could not understand. Here his thoughts were in a maze and in confusion. She loved him. He knew that now. He knew it! For just an instant that light which he had once told himself lay hidden in the depths of those brown eyes, that love-light he had yearned to see, had leaped into flame for him —*for him!* It brought him now a mad, surging rush of joy. She had not been able to hide it. She loved him. He had held her in his arms. He stretched out his arms now as though to take her, to crush her to him again. Anne! Anne! But she had said there could never be anything between them. What had she meant? What had she meant when she had said that she was not what he thought she was? What did it matter what she meant? Whatever it was, it should not stand between them now that he knew, now that he was sure her love was his!

It grew darker, and the smooth, undulating surface of the sea began to mirror tiny, shimmering lanes of light as the stars in their myriads began to sprinkle the heavens. And then into the darkness began to creep a soft and mellow glow—the moon was coming up.

Lane felt his arm grasped suddenly.

"Alola!" Ratu grunted—and pointed ahead.

Lane strained his eyes forward. At first he could see nothing; and then, finally, he made out a light— but it was so far away that, left to himself, he would not have noticed it at all.

He kept his eyes fixed upon it now. After a while he was certain that it was brighter. They were gaining, of course; he knew that; it was obvious since they had picked up the *Alola* at all, but—

Again his arm was grasped.

"Talimi!" grunted Ratu again—and once more pointed ahead.

Yes! He could see that! It looked like a black smudge on the sky line. He did not know how far away it was—too near, he was afraid, to give them time to overtake the *Alola* and reach it first.

Donald Lane was crouched forward now in his seat watching tensely. The *Alola's* light grew brighter; Talimi began to loom up out of the darkness and take shadowy form. They drew in closer —and suddenly the *Alola's* light was gone. He nodded in a sort of grim resignation to himself. She was rounding a point, heading in through the reefs for her anchorage inside the lagoon. She would make it first—that was beyond question now. But by very little! He began to recognize landmarks in the fuller moonlight. It was absolutely certain that he could not overtake her; but, at least, he could reach his uncle's house as soon as any one landing from the *Alola* could—before, for instance, his uncle could be inveigled into handing over the package to a thief.

He laughed out suddenly, harshly. The package was in the living-room behind the sliding panel. His uncle, everybody in the house probably, would have flocked down to meet the *Alola*—they always did when any boat came in. It was one of the big events in island life. Well, he could go and stand guard in the living-room—be there to *welcome* whoever was craftily imposing himself on John Crane!

The boat rounded the point. Still far ahead showed the *Alola's* light once more, and beyond again there came into view now a number of other lights, like tiny luminous pin points, where, some two miles away, he estimated, Talimi's principal group of houses bordered the edge of the lagoon. Between him and the anchorage, but much nearer the latter, was his uncle's house on a little rise of land that overlooked the lagoon itself.

The lights grew plainer, more distinct. The motor boat covered another mile, hugging in close to the shore now at Lane's gesticulated orders. The *Alola,* he made no doubt, had already dropped anchor; he could see a row of lights that he judged were from her portholes—as though she had swung around broadside to him. And, he was not sure, but there seemed to be another vessel there, too— at least he saw what looked like a riding light high up on a masthead.

His eyes now searched the shore abreast of him. Five minutes passed, another five; and then suddenly he touched Ratu on the shoulder and motioned him to head in directly for the beach. He was, as nearly as he could make out, just opposite his uncle's house.

The boat grounded on the sand. Lane thrust a generous sum of money into the native's hand, slapped the man in hearty approval upon the shoulder, and sprang ashore. Ratu would probably hobnob with his kind in Talimi for the rest of the night; in any case, the man needed no looking after.

Lane ran at top speed across the beach, and, a moment later, began to thread his way through a cocoanut grove. Just beyond, a few hundred yards away, he should, unless he had misjudged his landing, come out into the clearing where his uncle's house was built.

Yes, there it was! Through the trees he could see it now. It lay dark, shadowy in the moonlight that flooded the clearing. There was no light showing from any window. He nodded to himself. Of course! It was as he had expected. Everybody had gone down to the lagoon to meet the *Alola.*

He was just at the edge of the grove now—and suddenly he halted. The side of the low verandah where the wide French doors opened into the living-room faced him, but the overhang of the roof produced confusing shadows—and yet he was almost certain he had seen something move there—like a figure running swiftly in the direction of the living-room doors.

Lane's jaws clamped together. He ran silently, cautious of making any sound now, across the clearing. And now he could see that the living-room doors were open. He reached the verandah, and, tiptoeing noiselessly across it, gained the threshold of the living-room.

And then he stood spellbound—like a man dazed and suddenly bereft of reason. There was moonlight enough to see. The sliding panel was open, and a girl's figure stood before it; and from the opening she was in the act of withdrawing the brown paper package of jewels that had been intrusted to John Crane.

He felt himself sway unsteadily upon his feet. And then a great choking sound came from his lips. "Anne!" he heard himself cry out miserably.

CHAPTER XIV   IN WHICH THE WICKED PROSPER

THE package dropped from Anne's hands to the floor. Her lips moved, but she made no sound. In the moonlight her face was grey-white, bloodless.

Donald Lane stepped forward into the room toward her.

"You, Anne—*you!*" he said hoarsely.

She did not look at him—her face was crushed in her hands now.

He heard a sudden, broken sob.

"What does this mean, Anne?" he cried out desperately. "There must be some—some *other* explanation!"

Anne's little *figure* slowly drew itself erect. Her hands came away from her face—to clench tightly at her sides. There was agony in her eyes, but they were dry.

"There is no—no other explanation," she said in a low monotone.

Something stabbed with brutal hurt at Lane's heart. That letter pretending to have been written by Mrs. Thompson—by a woman—the ingenuity, so glaringly an evidence of premeditated guilt if it were true, invoked to overcome the inability to counterfeit a man's handwriting!

"It was you who wrote that letter I received in Kaliti—to keep me away from here?" he said in a dead voice.

"Yes," she answered.

"You wrote it in Mrs. Thompson's name because of the handwriting?"

"Yes," she said again.

He passed his hand wearily across his eyes.

"I came over in a motor boat—just made it, and no more," he said heavily. "How did you get off the *Alola* ahead of the others?"

"Does it matter?" she said with an effort. "It was dark when the *Alola* dropped anchor. It was not difficult to slip overside from the lower deck unobserved in the bustle of arrival—and it is only a short swim across the lagoon in this direction. It is very much shorter than by the road from the landing, and—and I didn't expect you, and I—I needed only two or three minutes. I should have been able to reach my own house and change before anybody got there."

She was wet. He realized that from the beginning he had been subconsciously aware her clothes had seemed to fit strangely upon her. She had evidently wrung out her skirts, for he saw no drip upon the floor—but her garments still clung closely to her.

"I left my shoes outside there," she said monotonously, "so as not to track any water in here." She was in her bare feet. He had not specifically noticed that, either. His mind was in torment.

A thief! That was what she had meant when she had said she was not what he thought she was. He closed his eyes for an instant and pressed both hands hard against them. There was bitter distress in his voice when he spoke again.

"How did you know about this?"—he jerked his hand toward the open panel. "And how did you know the package was there; and how did you know about the package in the first place?"

"I have known about the panel ever since I was a child," she answered. "I guessed the package was there. Your other question I refuse to answer."

A sudden gleam of hope came to Lane. If she were acting as a Soviet agent! Yes, why not? She wouldn't be a thief then. It might very easily be. Her father, say, had been employed by the Soviet Government, and Anne—

"You're trying to recover these for the Soviet Government, Anne!" he burst out eagerly. "That's it, isn't it? Your father was commissioned to do so in Europe, and you're helping him."

"No," she said, a sort of hopeless finality in her voice. "I know nothing about the Soviet Government, and my father does not know that I am here."

He turned away for a moment, sick at heart, trying to force his mind to think calmly.

"If it was you who wrote that letter, it must have been you who took that paper from my pocket last night."

"Yes," she said.

"How did you know I had it?"

"I refuse to answer that too," she said.

"What did you do with it?"

"I destroyed it," she answered.

Another gleam of hope came suddenly. If he could make her disprove her own statements! Prove her illogical out of her own mouth!

"If you intended to get here before any one from the *Alola* did, and intended to get that package before any one was able to interfere, what was the object in attempting to hold me over in Kaliti?"

144

She shook her head in a tired way.

"I was not sure I *could* get here first," she said. "But if you were not here, Monsieur Faradeau, since he did not have the paper, would not be given the package and be able to go away with it again on the *Alola,* and I would still have been able, when everybody had gone to bed, to get in here and take it."

"My God!" Donald Lane turned away again, his face white, haggard, drawn. A thief! Anne a thief! A clever one—every detail deliberately plotted out; mischance even, as far as possible, provided for!

And then suddenly he swung toward her, his arms stretched out.

"Anne," he cried out passionately, "say something—anything! Won't you give me a *chance* to disbelieve this!"

She stirred a little—swayed slightly against the wall. But her voice did not falter.

"There is nothing to say," she said.

Nothing to say! He was standing near the mantel. He crossed his arms upon it, and bowed his head. Nothing to say!

Presently he looked up. From the distance there came faintly the sound of voices.

"Some one is coming," he said dully.

There was a strange challenge in her eyes, a stiffening of the little figure, but she made no response.

Donald Lane's voice broke.

"I—I think you would better go," he said.

She did not answer him, did not look at him again; her face, averted, hid the sudden quiver of her lips; her bare feet made no sound as she crossed the room and went out through the open doors.

She was gone.

For a time Donald Lane stood motionless, like a man carved in stone, his eyes fixed on the spot in the moonlight just beyond the verandah where she had disappeared from view. He was conscious only now that something catastrophic had happened, that his mind rocked with turmoil, chaos, unendurable pain.

The sound of voices again, nearer, louder now, roused him. The package on the floor caught his eye. He stepped forward, picked it up, returned it to its hiding place, and closed the panel. Then he took a match from his pocket, struck it, and lighted a lamp.

A moment later John Crane appeared on the verandah. Behind

him was Monsieur Faradeau.

"Hello, Donald!" John Crane called out in amazement. "How'd you get here? I understood from Monsieur Faradeau here, and also from Captain Croon, that you were staying over in Kaliti in response to a letter you'd received from Thompson transmitting a request of mine to attend to some business with him—a request, incidentally, that I never made."

"I found that out," said Lane grimly. "That's why I'm here. I borrowed Thompson's motor boat."

Monsieur Faradeau came hurriedly forward, and caught Lane's hand effusively.

"Sacre nom!" he exclaimed. "But you are a man! This is good fortune for me! Monsieur Crane, your uncle, has been most kind. He has said that, after you arrived and our business was transacted, he would even send me to Sydney on his yacht, since the *Alola* would be gone, and that meanwhile I was to be his guest. Indeed, he is having my luggage brought up here; but, now that you have come, I can still go with the *Alola,* for it will not be until daylight that she sails."

"The yacht's back?" Lane asked; and, as John Crane nodded affirmatively: "I thought I saw a riding light in the lagoon." Then quickly: "Monsieur Faradeau, of course, has told you the story of his mission, and about the theft of the paper last night? I sent word to him to do so."

"Yes," said John Crane slowly. "And this little game that was played on you at Kaliti, but which you seem to have beaten, appears to be the second move in the attempt to rob Monsieur Faradeau and deceive me. But I can't quite understand what form it was to take—or is to take. If Monsieur Faradeau were out of the way, and the paper was presented to me by an impostor, the play would be obvious—but Monsieur Faradeau is here."

Donald Lane did not answer. He had once approached that problem in exactly the same way. He knew better now—knew that the play was over. Monsieur Faradeau and his package would not be interfered with again—but it seemed very trivial, that fact, bitterly trivial. Something else had been stolen, something of far greater moment, something out of his life, leaving it bare, and drab, and shapeless, was gone forever. It was something of which neither his uncle nor Monsieur Faradeau would ever know.

"Yes," said Monsieur Faradeau, "that is so. But it is all the more reason that I should, now that it is possible, go away at once with that package before whatever is to be attempted can be put into effect. It is certain that the package is not safe here any more. I can put it in Captain Croon's strong-box, and in Sydney deposit it in a safety vault while I am negotiating for its sale, as I have been instructed to do."

John Crane pulled thoughtfully at his tawny beard.

"Well, I suppose that's so," he said. Then abruptly: "Donald, Monsieur Faradeau says he gave a certain paper, since stolen, into your keeping. Could you swear that it was in my handwriting?"

"Absolutely!" Donald Lane replied emphatically. "There is no question about it whatever. Nor is there any question but that it is *the* paper, which, of course, I've known all about for weeks."

"This is not a light matter," said John Crane gravely. "You are sure that it corresponds with the other copy which we have here, and which you have seen?"

"I am sure," said Donald Lane as emphatically as before.

"That's all right, then," said John Crane quietly; "for I was satisfied that, so far as his story was concerned, Monsieur Faradeau's identity could not be disputed." He stepped over to the verandah doors, and shut them; then he opened the sliding panel, and took out the brown paper parcel. "Here it is," he said—and handed it to Monsieur Faradeau.

"Monsieur Crane," said Monsieur Faradeau with emotion, "I do not know how to thank you— not only for myself, but for the others. We are all very grateful to you."

"Tush!" said John Crane heartily. "Nothing to it at all, man! It was little enough to do for a friend such as Martin Todd. We'll open that package now, and check it up." He thrust his hand inside the panel again, felt around for a moment, and brought out a slip of paper. "Here's the other list."

"Monsieur," said Monsieur Faradeau earnestly,

"I do not question the—"

"Open it, anyway," laughed John Crane. "I might be handing you a package of old nails. I checked it up when I got it; we'll check it up now when I hand it back."

Monsieur Faradeau opened the package.

Donald Lane whistled low under his breath. He had never seen the contents before.

"Worth a lot of money, eh, Donald?" grunted John Crane, as the light fell on the glittering array of precious stones. "But the best of them all is— this!" He held up the pearl necklace. "If you had a girl, Donald"—he grinned quizzically—"I'd be almost tempted to make Monsieur Faradeau an offer for it."

"Thanks!" said Lane shortly. "You're quite safe."

The items comprising the package were checked, and the package tied up again.

"You're quite sure you've decided to go back on board the *Alola*, Monsieur Faradeau?" John Crane asked hospitably. "Any friend of Martin Todd is welcome in this house as long as he will stay."

"I thank you," said Monsieur Faradeau, with a grateful smile; "but I am certain the best thing for me to do is to get back on board. I wonder, though"—he glanced inquiringly at Donald Lane— "if, since I have this with me, Monsieur Lane would be good enough to walk back with me to the ship? I would feel safer."

"Certainly, I will!" agreed Lane promptly.

"Then I'll go now," said Monsieur Faradeau. "Afterwards I am sure you will have a great deal to say to each other, and I would only be intruding."

"Not at all!" said John Crane pleasantly. "But do just as you like. I'll send the boys back with your things."

Monsieur Faradeau shook hands with John Crane, expressed again his deep gratitude to the other, and, accompanied by Donald Lane, set out on the return journey to the *Alola*. He talked constantly—he mingled renewed assurances of his gratitude with accounts of experiences in Russia.

Donald Lane was in no mood for conversation— he was even an inattentive listener.

At the shore of the lagoon they parted, as Monsieur Faradeau stepped into a native boat and was rowed out to the *Alola*.

Donald Lane watched the boat until it reached the *Alola's* side, then he turned and began to retrace his steps slowly to the house. But halfway back along the road, he branched off suddenly and sat down in a moonlit patch of woods. He was in no mood for conversation with his uncle either.

Time passed. He sat there on a fallen tree trunk, his chin gripped in his hands—gripped so tightly at times that he left abrasions, little purple marks, upon the skin of his jowls. His face was colourless.

"Anne!" he said once aloud. "Oh, my God— Anne!"

In the moonlight, long after, he looked at his wrist watch. It was far past midnight. He had been there two hours.

CHAPTER XV   THE BREAKING POINT

ANNE opened her eyes, and looked around her. She was conscious of a soft, filmy light that was broken into queer little shafts and patches, while everywhere else there seemed to be an innumerable number of tall, black shadows, some of which moved and some of which stood very still. She moaned a little and lifted her head from the ground, and passed her hands feebly across her eyes. That was moonlight, wasn't it? and the black shadows were trees? But where was she? She could not seem to remember anything— but— but in the place of memory was an overpowering sense of dread, of terror—as of some dire thing that was impending and from which there was no escape—or else something that had already happened and whose horror, though it was nameless, still hung over her, and—

With a sudden cry of anguish, she raised herself weakly to her feet—and then stood swaying, clutching at a tree-trunk to hold herself erect. Yes, she remembered now—she remembered. But she was very weak—she had no strength and a horrible sense of dizziness was creeping upon her—her head swam giddily.

Perhaps she would be better in a moment or so— if she stood very still.

She stared ahead of her along one of the little patches or moonlight, to where, breaking through the tree-trunks, it flooded the road with mellow radiance. That *was* the road out there wasn't it? Yes, she remembered now! She remembered that she had been running—running wildly, her eyes full of tears running as though she were trying to escape from *herself.* She remembered that suddenly the moonlight had vanished, that a vast darkness which swirled and swirled around her had taken its place, and that she had swerved blindly, and was stumbling in brush and undergrowth—and then unconsciousness had come.

It had been a very merciful unconsciousness. If —if it could only have endured—for—for always! No! Not yet—not yet. There was something still to do. Perhaps afterwards! It would be a boon then.

She held very tightly to the tree-trunk, but her hands seemed to be slipping. She half slid, half fell to the ground. Oh, yes, she knew! She had been barely convalescent, just out of bed when she had left Fiji, and since then—oh, why—why must she think of *that!* And then that swim to-night. It had been so long, so terribly, terribly long, and it had seemed that she would never reach the shore. And it had not been far—not nearly so far as the distances she had swum even as a little girl, many and many a time here in the lagoon, and—and thought it only fun.

Her lips moved.

". . . Donald . . . Oh, Donald . . ."

Blackness—the merciful nothingness was coming again.

The moonlight fell once more upon a figure in wet, sodden garments, a figure huddled with its face upon the ground, a figure that lay so still it seemed like the great quiet and the great stillness of one dead.

Presently she stirred again. At first her mind was blank—and then the surge of memory came once more. She must get up. She must go on. There was something still to do. Again she struggled to her feet, and again, swaying, clutched at the tree-trunk for support. She would be stronger in a moment—just a moment to get her strength back, and then she would go on again. It couldn't be very far, for she must already have come nearly all the way home. *Home!* She cried out involuntarily, and with a shudder, closed her eyes. The word was a cruel mockery! *Home!*

She must not think of that. She had far too little strength left to think of anything but what she had to do. There was still the package. Her father should never have it—*never!* It wasn't the end yet. It was very near the end, perhaps, very near—but if God would give her just a little strength she would go on.

That was what had been in her mind when she had run—so long, long ago now, it seemed—from John Crane's house back there, and had left Donald standing in the living-room, his face chalky white, bloodless, like a ghost's in the moonlight staring after a retreating thief.

Thief!

Anne dug her fingers into the bark of the tree until the pain of it caused her mechanically to relax her hold. Donald knew her as a thief, had seen her as a thief, had heard her *confess* it. That was the price she paid, and he—

She *must* not think of anything except what she had to do. John Crane would give the package to that masquerading Frenchman, and Faradeau would bring it to her father's house—that was what they had arranged to do in Fiji. Some time tonight, before morning, before the

Alola sailed again, the package would be there. Perhaps it was there now. She had no means of knowing how long she had lain here unconscious in the woods. In some way—her wits must find *the* way when she got to the house—she would get possession of the package; or else, if not by her wits, then, as a last resort, coming unexpectedly upon them with her revolver, she would force her father and Faradeau to give it up to her.

And afterwards? Yes, yes! She knew what she would do then—there was only one thing she could do. She could *hide* the package. Then she would go to John Crane and say that she had stolen it from Faradeau, and—and Donald would bear her out in the statement that she was a thief—but she would not give the package to John Crane because he would only give it back to Faradeau again. She would only give it up to Martin Todd. Martin Todd must come for it. That was the only way—*nothing* would make her tell where it was.

Yes, she *was* stronger now. She took a step forward—and with a low, startled gasp, drew instantly back again. Some one was out there on the road. She heard the sound of footsteps, but, queerly, they seemed to come first from one direction and then from the opposite one. Her mind, faltering, weak, stumbled in confusion over this apparent contradiction, and then she understood. There were two people out there, and they were walking toward each other.

There came then a low whistle—twice repeated. It was answered from the other direction. And then two figures came suddenly into view and halted on the roadway almost in front of her. In the moonlight and through the trees Anne could see them distinctly. One was her father, and the other was the self-styled Monsieur Faradeau.

Monsieur Faradeau carried a small travelling bag in his hand.

Their voices reached her.

"Where have you been?" demanded Henry Walton sharply. "You've got it, haven't you?"

"Yes—here," Monsieur Faradeau answered.

"Well, you're infernally late," complained Henry Walton. "I was just going to look you up."

"I can't help it," replied Monsieur Faradeau gruffly. "I was supposed to go back to the *Alola* according to my story, and I wasn't taking any chances of pulling a bone, so I got Lane to walk along with me so that he would see me go aboard. It would have been all right then and I'd have been right back here, but that old fool of a skipper

152

spotted me, and there was nothing for it but to go to his cabin for a yarn and a drink. It's no wonder I'm late."

"Well, all right," said Henry Walton. "You're here now, and fortunately there's still plenty of time before the *Alola* sails again at daybreak." Then, abruptly: "Have you seen or heard anything of Anne?"

"Anne?" repeated Monsieur Faradeau In surprise. "No. Why?"

"Because I haven't, either," said Henry Walton shortly. "She didn't come ashore from the *Alola* with me, and I couldn't find her anywhere on board."

"That's queer," said Monsieur Faradeau. "Of course, I came ashore before you did, seeing that we weren't travelling in company just then on account of *Mister* John Crane, but I'm sure I saw her on deck just as the *Alola* anchored. Hasn't she been home?"

"I told you, didn't I, that I haven't seen her, and can't find her?" returned Henry Walton, caustically. "No, she hasn't been home."

"Well, then," said Monsieur Faradeau indifferently, "I fancy she had enough last night, and she's quit."

"The trouble with Anne"—an ugly purr had crept into Henry Walton's voice—"is that she never quits. You say there was no sign of her around John Crane's house, or any mention of her having been there?"

"Not an earthly!" said Monsieur Faradeau emphatically. "But, anyway, what's the good of worrying about her? She can't do anything more now, for we've got the swag. And as for herself she's bound to turn up when she gets good and ready. I'm not saying when that will be, though, for I don't think she is particularly crazy about her home or her dear father any more."

"Come along to the house," said Mr. Henry Walton laconically.

The two men passed out of sight down the road.

Anne took a step forward—and sank to her knees. She struggled up again. She must go on. It wasn't far to the house—just a little way—and they would be there with the package. Why was it that her limbs refused to obey her? She was on her knees again. And the moonlight was fading again. And strange sounds were in her ears.

Who was that screaming? Yes—of course! It was horrible—but it was Franchon, of course, staggering up a flight of stone steps.

And there was Mère Gigot . . . And Madame Frigon drinking out of a bottle so that she could hurl it out of her attic window at some

one on the street below . . . And the girl Tisotte who had been killed .
. . And Fire-Eyes with enormous amber-lensed eye-glasses instead of
a black beard . . . And a wounded Englishman who staggered along a
dark, narrow lane, and leaned upon her for support, and whose weight
was growing heavier and heavier, so heavy that it was crushing her
down, and, though she must go on, she was sinking under it, lower
and lower . . .

And darkness . . .

Anne pitched forward to the ground.

CHAPTER XVI   JOHN CRANE PAYS A VISIT

A LIGHT was still burning in the living-room when Donald Lane, on his return, came in sight of the house again. His uncle, then, was still sitting up, waiting for him! His lips compressed a little. Of all men, his uncle was the one he did not want to talk to to-night, and now, with a prolonged absence to explain that, to say the least of it, was rather extraordinary, he had made matters worse. Well, he would have to see it through —make some casual excuse—and, for the rest, keep the conversation on the safe topic of business.

He stepped on to the verandah, and walked toward the living-room doors—but halted on the threshold, as a native servant came hurriedly forward and handed him an unaddressed, sealed envelope.

The blood suddenly began to pound fiercely in its course through Lane's veins. It was perhaps from Anne! Who else could it be from? But why —why should she write? A miserably appalling thought flashed through his brain. Not that—she hadn't done *that*!—because she was desperate, trapped, and could see no other way out! For an instant he was afraid to open the envelope.

He glanced inside the living-room. It was empty. Then he tore the envelope open, and stared in a stunned way at the half-dozen scrawled words that met his eyes:

Come at once to Walton's house.

JOHN CRANE.

It wasn't from Anne—it wasn't what he had been afraid of, thank God! But his uncle at Henry Walton's! The men hadn't spoken to each other for years! His mind began to run riot.

"How long since Mr. Crane left here?" he demanded brusquely of the servant.

The man answered rapidly in the native tongue.

Lane shook his head impatiently. He had not been long enough in the islands to gain even a smattering of the language. He could not understand.

The native repeated what he had said—then suddenly grinned, and, running into the living-room, placed his finger on the dial of the clock.

"Ten minutes ago!" Lane ejaculated. "All right!"

He turned abruptly, jumped from the verandah, and regained the

155

road. And now he ran at top speed. It was a little more than a mile to Henry Walton's place. Perhaps he could get there as soon as his uncle did, or perhaps even overtake the other —for John Crane would certainly not run. It was Anne who was in his thoughts. Had she been seen in his uncle's house, seen at the panel, by some one besides himself—a native servant, perhaps, who had reported it to John Crane? It must be something like that. No ordinary thing would take John Crane to Henry Walton's house! And if she had been seen! What then? What could he do?

His laugh suddenly rang hollow as he ran. He didn't know what he could do. He didn't even know why he ran, since, in the last analysis, even if he refused to speak, his silence itself would only corroborate whatever other evidence of her guilt there might be. No; he had it now! It was not to reach Anne that he ran. It was to reach his uncle first; to plead with his uncle to let the matter drop without a word to Anne—to save her that. Faradeau had his damned jewels now! That was enough! That ended it!

He came in sight of Henry Walton's house. There was only one light showing—a light that came through the interstices of the outer, slatted door of one of the rooms that opened on the verandah. He had not caught up with his uncle—the native's "ten minutes" had probably been anything but reliable—but the house was quite close to the road, and he could see now what looked like the forms of several men grouped outside the door on the verandah through which came the narrow streaks of light.

There was a short stretch of lawn in front of the house. Lane started to cross this, but halted suddenly as one of the group on the verandah, evidently catching sight of him, came quickly forward in his direction—and a moment later he could see that it was John Crane.

He waited for his uncle to join him.

"Saw you coming and was afraid you'd make a noise," said John Crane in a whisper. "Come along —and not a sound, remember, especially on the verandah."

"But what's up? What's the matter?" demanded Lane.

"You'll see in a minute," John Crane answered. "No time to tell you now."

Anne! Yes, it must be that they had found out! It couldn't be anything else; and, worse still, his uncle had brought others into it too—there were two men there on the verandah.

"But, look here, uncle"—Lane's voice was anxious—"Before you go any farther with this, I—"

"Come along!" interrupted John Crane briskly— and, turning, started back for the verandah again.

Lane followed—there was nothing else to do. He crossed the verandah. The others made room for him before the door of the lighted room.

At a nudge from his uncle, Lane leaned forward a little reluctantly to peer in through the slats—and the next instant he hung there tense, amazed and confounded at what he saw. Inside, on the floor of the room, lay a discarded piece of brown wrapping-paper; spread out upon a table and resting on a bed of white cotton, a magnificent array of jewelled ornaments scintillated in the light; at the table sat Mr. Henry Walton and Monsieur Faradeau. Between the two men was a dice-box, and directly in front of each of them was an individual little heap of jewels. And now, as Lane watched, Mr. Henry Walton picked up the dice-box, shook it, rolled the dice on the table—and passed the box to Monsieur Faradeau. Monsieur Faradeau went through the same pantomime. Mr. Henry Walton grinned, studied the central heap of ornaments attentively for an instant, and then, selecting one, added it to his individual pile. Monsieur Faradeau in turn did likewise.

"Good God!" Lane muttered under his breath. "Splitting the swag by dicing for first choice each time"—there was a snarl in John Crane's whisper— "but I'll bet it's Walton's idea, and that the dice are loaded. But we've seen enough! If you've got the door unlocked, Fleming, let's carry on!"

"Right!" Lane heard the man at his elbow whisper back. "Stand aside a little!"

It seemed to Lane, his mind still in confusion and amaze, that the thing had happened in a flash— the door was flung violently open, and he found himself standing inside the room with his companions.

The voice of the man who had broken in the door rang out sharply:

"I'm Fleming, of the Sydney police, gentlemen!" He was covering the two men at the table with a revolver. "Hardly worth while to make trouble, I think!"

Monsieur Faradeau gave a startled cry; Mr. Henry Walton half rose from his chair—and dropped back again with a phlegmatic shrug of his shoulders.

"Perhaps not," drawled Henry Walton; "but this is a bit high-handed, isn't it—breaking into my house? However, I see my *friend,* Mr. Crane, there—perhaps that explains it."

"Yes!" Crane's voice boomed out suddenly. "It does!"

"It's a long time since I have had the honour of a visit!" Henry Walton drawled again. "Too bad you should have judged me so harshly all these years, and robbed me of the pleasure of your society, and all over no more than a native girl who—but she's dead now, poor thing! *De mortuis nil nisi*—"

"You damned swine!" roared John Crane furiously. "As fine a little girl as ever lived, and you as good as killed her, you—you—" His voice broke; he took a step forward. "I—"

Anne! Where was Anne? Lane, fighting for his own composure, caught his uncle's arm.

"Steady, uncle!" he said in a low voice. "No good in that!"

The man who had described himself as Fleming, of the Sydney police, was still covering the two men at the table. He spoke now gruffly.

"I arrest you both," he said, "for the robbery of those jewels from the Paris branch of Kingsley, Mertlewaite and Company of London."

CHAPTER XVII   THE CARDS ARE FACED

DONALD LANE was the only man in the room who moved; there was a sudden choking sensation in his throat, and his fingers sought and tugged at his collar-band. He stared at the two men at the table.

"It's a lie!" shouted Monsieur Faradeau. "It's a lie!"

"Quite a famous establishment!" observed Henry Walton, with an ironical smile. "You've chosen quite the most famous jewellers in Europe, I should say!"

"It's a lie!' repeated Monsieur Faradeau violently. "Monsieur Crane, there, knows quite well where these things came from. They were sent to him by his friend Monsieur Martin Todd."

Donald Lane heard a voice speak quietly from behind him.

"I am Martin Todd," it said.

Lane swung sharply around. It was the third man who had been outside on the verandah. Monsieur Faradeau's jaw dropped.

"I never saw you before!" he muttered.

"That is *exactly* the point," said Martin Todd.

"You're a bit of a fool, Faradeau!" murmured Henry Walton caustically. His eyes appeared to rest speculatively for an instant on the dice-box, then he smiled calmly around the circle. "However, your—er—confession makes little difference—I fancy the jig's up. But just how this pleasant little denouement has come about is not quite clear in my mind."

"Then, I'll tell you!" said John Crane harshly. "Two weeks—"

"Just a minute!" interrupted Fleming, of the Sydney police. "Stand up, you two!" he ordered coldly; and then, as he was obeyed: "Mr. Todd, would you mind going through them for arms while I keep them covered?"

Lane's brain was whirling. Anne's father was in this! He found himself repeating that phrase continually to himself. It seemed a hopelessly damning sort of thing—and a chance word would bring Anne in, too. He saw a revolver taken from each of the men. Fleming had drawn a pair of handcuffs from his pocket. The room was hot, stifling—Lane tugged with his fingers at his collar-band again. The sweat was standing out in beads on his forehead. Queer, that no one else seemed to find the heat unbearable! Anne's father had his right wrist locked to Monsieur Faradeau's left.

"I think"—Henry Walton's voice came cool and utterly unmoved—"you were interrupted, Mr. Crane?"

"Yes," snapped John Crane; "but to good purpose! Two weeks ago my yacht, that had been in Sydney for repairs, came back to Talimi. It brought Mr. Todd here, who had come out to this part of the world on a visit to his old haunts, and, being in Sydney and learning that my yacht was leaving for Talimi, decided to come back on her to spend a few weeks with me. I supposed, when I first saw him, that he had come in person for the package of jewels, for up to that time I had had no suspicion that anything was wrong. I"—he smiled grimly—"had not been aware until then that the Paris jewel robbery had been the talk of the Continent for a week after it had been perpetrated, as during that particular week I was on my yacht en route from Havre to New York, and we were unable to establish any communication or receive any messages."

Henry Walton waved his free hand airily.

"A tribute to Monsieur Faradeau," he said softly. "Monsieur Faradeau is amazingly clever in such matters. I am afraid he stole aboard that night at Havre and tampered rather effectually with the yacht's wireless—"

"Yes!" said John Crane curtly. "That also became clear. I immediately sent the yacht back to Sydney to report to police headquarters. A cable was sent to Paris for a list of the stolen articles, and Inspector Fleming here came back on the yacht. We compared the cabled description with the contents of the package, found them to correspond— and then waited for the next move. It was obvious that it must come through the medium of the *Alola,* not necessarily on this trip, but on some trip, for there was no other way of reaching Talimi. I met the *Alola* to-night, while Mr. Todd and Fleming kept in the background. We were afraid that the sight of Mr. Todd particularly might warn our quarry off before giving us a chance to recognize it! We were rewarded by Monsieur Faradeau's introduction of himself. The result is that we are here!"

"Thank you!" said Henry Walton pleasantly. "It explains—er—partially."

Martin Todd was a heavy-built, red-faced man, and obviously choleric of temper. He banged his fist suddenly upon the table.

"I want to know how the devil you brought me into this?" he snapped.

"Oh, that!" Henry Walton shrugged his shoulders. "It is almost childishly simple, isn't it? The actual robbery was a mere bagatelle. The real problem was to get the loot out of the country without any trace of it being left behind, and get it somewhere where every police officer wasn't hunting for it, and every 'fence' afraid of it. I'd had my eyes on the job for quite a while, and" —he turned suddenly to John Crane—"I'd thought of you and your yacht too, Crane, in connection with it— for quite a while! Rather a bit of a joke on you, wouldn't you say? Thought under the circumstances you wouldn't mind the liberty! It was merely a question of waiting for one of your periodical visits to Havre—and capitalizing the intimacy that, when you and I used to walk about the island here with our arms around each other's neck, you told me existed between Martin Todd and yourself."

Neither Martin Todd nor John Crane made any response.

Fleming, who had been staring at Henry Walton's face, spoke abruptly:

"There's still another of you in this; a chap who called himself Kendall—the one who took the package to Mr. Crane. Where is he?"

"Dead," said Henry Walton.

"Dead—eh?" said Fleming sharply. "Well, we'll investigate that!"

"As you will," said Henry Walton indifferently. "It is none the less true. There's not the slightest object in hiding it now. Kendall was a very clever man, one of the cleverest in his—er—profession; but he had the rather grave fault of being over-ambitious. On the night after he got back from Havre, he ran foul of the police on a little affair of his own, entirely unconnected with this one save for the fact that he still had in his pocket the paper, the—er—credentials, he had received from Mr. Crane the night before. He was shot when running away from the police, but evaded them though he was badly wounded; and, being afraid that he would either still be caught, or perhaps picked up in an unconscious condition, he succeeded—I am sure the details would not interest you!—in mailing the paper to me. Eventually, he managed to take refuge in a somewhat ill-famed dive run by one Mère Gigot. He died at Mère Gigot's that night. I"—Henry Walton smiled slightly—"must be honest enough to admit I did not mourn him—it left two, Monsieur Faradeau and myself, to share, instead of three."

"I see!" said Fleming. "Well, I'll say you've a loving disposition anyway!" He stepped suddenly to the edge of the table, and, as suddenly, leaning forward, snatched the pince-nez from Henry Walton's nose. And then for a long minute he stared intently again into the other's face. "By heavens, I know who you are now!" he burst out. "You are Peter Railler, alias a dozen other names, the Holsgate bank-thief who escaped from Dartmoor, and who we caught and held in Sydney while we waited for Marston of the Yard to come out and take you back! You were supposed to have gone down with the *Kandahar* sixteen years ago!"

Donald Lane mechanically sought to ease his collar-band again. Anne! Back of all this was Anne. There was something immeasurably wretched about the whole business. What a change, what a startling change, the man's eyes made in his appearance once those amber-lensed glasses were off! And for the first time the man's self-possession was shaken. Just for a moment, though; just a slight loss of colour, a barely perceptible twitching of the lips—and then a bland smile again. His sang-froid was amazing. Not like Faradeau! Faradeau was hunched up in his seat, his face colourless, his jaw hanging loosely, his eyes roving around the room like a hunted animal's.

Henry Walton's voice came with smooth imperturbability:

"I had perhaps a little the advantage of you, Fleming. I recognized you the moment you entered the room. The—er—obvious does not admit denial, does it? I am John Railler. Well"—he shrugged his shoulders—"I'm out of luck—for the moment. Would it be too much to ask why you did not arrest my friend Faradeau the moment he presented himself?—You—er—hardly expected he would lead you *here.*"

It was John Crane who answered—raspingly.

"No," he said, "in spite of knowing you for a cur and from every moral standpoint as a murderer, you are the last man I would have suspected. We knew there were others besides Faradeau in this; and we knew that some one else was here in Talimi on the same mission that he was—but, so far as we could make out, the 'some one else' was trying to double-cross Faradeau. We gave Faradeau a little rope, and used him for bait. He was watched from the moment he went back on board the *Alola.*"

"You thought he was being double-crossed, of course," said Henry Walton, "because his paper was stolen from him last night?"

"Not only that," John Crane answered tersely; "but because an attempt was made to keep my nephew here from reaching Talimi to-night." Henry Walton smiled quizzically.

"Oh! I see!" He broke into low laughter.

"Amusing to the last! Poor Anne! She—"

He stopped abruptly. Donald Lane had sprung forward to the edge of the table, his face set and white, his fists clenched until the knuckles showed like rows of ivory knobs across the back of his hands.

And for a moment the eyes of the two men met and held each other's.

It was Henry Walton who spoke.

"Ah!" he said calmly. "Of course! Mr. Lane! I quite understand your feelings, but I was merely going to say that Anne is quite innocent of any intentional wrong-doing; she has, on the contrary, been —er—impetuous even in her virtue."

"What do you mean?" demanded Lane hoarsely.

"Anne, I regret to say," said Henry Walton, in the same conversational tones, "overheard Faradeau and myself discussing this affair the night before last in the bungalow at Fiji. She was very much distressed at discovering herself to be the daughter of a criminal—to a large extent, I fancy, on account of the fact that she had recently fallen in love. She was given the alternative of sacrificing the life of the gentleman of her choice—you, Mr. Lane—or giving a pledge to say nothing of what she had overheard. She chose the latter—and salved her conscience by reserving to herself the right to prevent us, if she could do so by her own efforts, from going any further with our— er—little plans."

"Do you mean to say," Donald Lane shouted out —and in sudden fury stumbled for his words, "do you mean to say that—that I—that you threatened Anne with harm to me?"

"Why, yes—which she would share, of course," said Henry Walton—and stifled a yawn with his free hand. "Pardon me! Your lives were not of the same value to me as, I imagine, you regard them yourselves—and certainly, at a hundred thousand pounds, were luxuries far beyond what I could afford."

The man seemed to be wholly devoid of emotion. There was no questioning the fact that he meant exactly what he said—he exuded a sense of utter, inhuman disregard for every moral obligation.

Donald Lane gripped at the table edge. His brain was in tumult. Anne! To—to save him! And he—

"Who is this Anne?" demanded Fleming, of the Sydney police, abruptly. "Whose daughter is she?"

"His own," John Crane answered shortly.

"My word!" ejaculated Fleming. "She must be a precocious child to fall in love and take a hand in this sort of thing at the age of—well, say, fifteen at the very most."

"Anne is not a child," John Crane grunted, with a short laugh. "She is a young woman of nineteen or twenty."

There was a strange silence for a moment. Donald Lane found himself staring from Fleming to Henry Walton and back again. The eyes of the two men were holding each other's fixedly.

And then Henry Walton, with a slight shrug of his shoulders, smiled faintly.

"Fleming," he murmured, "you should rise high in your profession!"

"It's a matter of simple arithmetic," Fleming answered curtly. "She couldn't be your daughter. If she is nineteen or twenty, she was three or four years old when the *Kandahar* went down sixteen years ago. You were on the *Kandahar,* a prisoner in charge of Marston on your way back to Dartmoor, and you are the first one out of all on board who has ever been heard of since that disaster. For six years previous to that you were in Dartmoor— serving a twenty-year sentence when you escaped. She couldn't be your daughter. Who is she?"

Again Henry Walton shrugged his shoulders. "Apart from the fact that, besides myself, she is the only survivor of the *Kandahar* I know of, I haven't the slightest idea."

Donald Lane cried out sharply.

"Anne's not your daughter, you say!" There was a strange, broken eagerness in his voice. "You say she was saved with you from the *Kandahar!* How? Tell me how!"

Henry Walton eyed Lane for a moment half quizzically, half tolerantly.

"No reason why I shouldn't," he drawled finally. "We were in the purser's boat—a lot of us. It was bad weather when the *Kandahar* took fire. A good many never got into any of the boats at all. I don't know how many days we were in the boat——I never knew. At the end it drifted ashore on an island where there were only natives. The only ones alive by that time were the child and myself—and there wasn't much life in us. We were taken care of in a native village. We stayed there a year—it was a delightfully secluded spot—and afterwards, well— er—I made a fresh start. The purser's box had a few thousand pounds in it, and—"

"And with a 'daughter' to bolster up your new identity, and the past wiped out by your supposed death, you became Mr. Henry Walton of Talimi and Paris, and started in at your old game again," cut in Fleming, of the Sydney police, evenly. "I can quite see why you made no effort to find out who she was; but even now, after all these years, it won't take long to do so—a reference to the passenger list of the *Kandahar,* that must still exist in the steamship offices, will put us on the track. A baby girl, three or four years old, is—"

"I would suggest," interrupted Henry Walton with a queer smile, as he leaned abruptly forward in his chair, "that something more immediate than that be done for her. She has had a very trying time during the last two days, and she was barely convalescent when the *Alola* left Suva. I am afraid that she has been listening again, and that it has been a little too much for her!" He pointed suddenly to the doorway. "Look!"

Donald Lane swung around—and then, with a cry that, surging from his soul, gave voice to an agony of distress, to fear, and love, and a great contrition, he sprang across the room. A figure was standing in the doorway—no, not standing, swaying there; a figure whose face was drawn and ashen grey, whose eyes were fixed in an expressionless stare; a figure whose hands, clutching at the door jamb for support, were slipping nervelessly from their hold.

"Anne!" he cried out.

There was a low, dull, ugly thud, as, before he could reach her, she went down in a crumpled heap upon the floor.

And then he was beside her.

"Anne!" he cried again, and gathered her up in his arms. "Oh, my God! Anne! Anne!"

He was conscious of commotion, of voices around him—but only in a detached, extraneous way. There was a couch across the room, and he carried her there and laid her tenderly down upon it. Some one brought water. He fell to bathing her face, to chafing her hands.

Cold fear clutched at his heart. She gave no sign of returning consciousness. She had not merely fainted—he *knew* that. It was more than that. Mind and body had been tortured beyond the breaking point—far beyond it.

"Get the doctor! Get the doctor at once!" His voice echoed in a hollow way in his own ears.

John Crane's voice answered him:

"I'll go myself."

A long time passed. There was no good chafing her hands—it didn't do any good—or the water didn't either. He looked around him. The room was empty. Everybody was gone. He didn't remember hearing them go.

He flung himself on his knees beside the couch, and buried his face in his hands. He knew an anguish that tore at his soul; an anguish bitter with its flood of self-reproach, unendurable with the fear that she—that she—oh, God, not that!—that she was so ill she would never look at him or smile at him again. His anguish! What was *his* anguish to what she must have suffered—the drear hopelessness, the shame that must have broken her heart! A thief! She had let him think her that—for his own sake.

He raised his head suddenly. She had moved a little—a deep breath like a long, weary sigh came from her.

"Anne—dear heart!" his voice trembled with eager hope. "You are better, dear?"

Her eyes were open—but there was no light of recognition in them. Her lips moved. He bent over her to catch the words.

"Broken waters!" she whispered—and stretched out her hands as one groping in darkness. "Broken waters! And, oh, Donald, I love you so!"

"We're through them, Anne! There are no broken waters any more! We're through them!" he cried. "It's all right now! Don't you know me, Anne? It's Donald!"

She made no answer—and he knew she had not heard him.

He buried his face again.

After a time, a hand fell in a kindly way upon his shoulder.

He looked up sharply. It was the doctor—and the doctor was smilingly indicating the door.

"Yes," said Lane hoarsely. "But you'll let me know—at once?"

"Right!" the doctor answered.

Lane stumbled across the room, and went out on the verandah.

John Crane came to him.

And somehow Donald Lane realized that, until now, he had never

166

known this man, his uncle, who, with an arm thrown around his shoulders and without a word, kept pace with him up and down the verandah.

Presently the doctor came.

"No need for anxiety," he said cheerily—and went back into the room again.

A great sob of thankfulness rose in Donald Lane's throat.

John Crane swore gruffly under the urge of emotion and relief.

"Known her since she was a little kiddie!" he spluttered. "She's the one I was thinking of in spite of that scoundrel—the one with the sunrise in her eyes the way it comes up off old Talimi here."

But Donald Lane made no answer. He was listening to a glad paean that was sounding in his soul, to a refrain that, set to music triumphant, seemed to well from nature herself and fill all the star-lit night with glory, and exquisite beauty—and a great peace:

"Oh, Donald, I love you so! . . . Oh, Donald, I love you so! . . ."

THE END.
[64300 WORDS]

www.ingramcontent.com/pod-product-compliance
Lightning Source LLC
Chambersburg PA
CBHW020617250626
47154CB00004B/1545